M. E. Francis

In a North Country Village

M. E. Francis

In a North Country Village

ISBN/EAN: 9783337230074

Printed in Europe, USA, Canada, Australia, Japan

Cover: Foto ©Andreas Hilbeck / pixelio.de

More available books at **www.hansebooks.com**

In a North Country Village

M. E. FRANCIS

(MRS. FRANCIS BLUNDELL)

AUTHOR OF

*"A DAUGHTER OF THE SOIL," "STORY OF DAN," "FRIEZE
AND FUSTIAN," &c.*

ILLUSTRATED BY FRANK FELLOES

.

OSGOOD, McILVAINE & CO.

45 ALBEMARLE STREET, W.

1897

CONTENTS

	Page
Thornleigh . . .	1
Gaffer's Child . .	21
Celebrities . . .	47
Naucy .	71
Politics . . .	103
The Gilly-F'ers .	117
Aunt Jinny	145
On the Other Side of the Wall . .	171
Little Paupers . .	191
Here and There . .	209
" Our Joe " . . ,	231
Mates	249

THORNLEIGH

THORNLEIGH

WE hear so much nowadays about the difficulties of agriculture, the increasing number of unlet farms, the exodus of the labourer, the fall of prices, and the growing spirit of radicalism, that we have come to think the typical British rustic, honest Farmer John Bull, as much a product of a bygone age as his once familiar red waistcoat and top-boots. On the other hand, the population of our large towns overflows their slums and alleys, and rows of hideous, ill-built houses start up on their outskirts and creep out further and further into the country until the fair green face of the land is seamed and disfigured by a very network of staring red brick. When one unduly prolongs one's walks or drives

3

in these populous districts, one wonders sometimes if the prognostications of certain mournful prophets will be realised in our days, and if our English villages, with their rugged, good-humoured inhabitants, their snug homesteads, their antiquated customs, will be altogether swept away.

And yet within eight miles of one of our largest Northern manufacturing towns, on the main road between it and a fashionable watering-place, there is a certain sleepy little hamlet that I know of, which has remained unchanged to all intents and purposes for several hundred years, and the inhabitants of which have lived there from generation to generation in undisturbed content.

There is but one rambling street, if street it can be called, where the houses are of all shapes and sizes, and stand at irregular distances from each other and from the road. If you chanced to stroll through Thornleigh on a summer's noontide you would think the whole place was asleep—not even a dog in sight, except, perhaps, where here and there in a large farm-yard one may be seen blinking in the sunshine outside his kennel with his muzzle between his outstretched paws. Even the hens cluck drowsily to their wandering broods, and the cats sit sunning themselves on the snowy doorsteps, watching with lazy upturned eyes the swallows that circle and twitter over their heads, or the amorous

pigeons that walk up and down on the tiled roofs opposite, bowing and cooing and "courtin'," as the good
folk here would call it, with equal affectation, and perseverance.   But the inhabitants of Thornleigh are
neither absent nor asleep; twelve o'clock is "dinner-

time" and they are all busy at their "mate."   There
is a fine odour of bacon in the air just now—bacon is
the staff of life at Thornleigh—for breakfast in the
morning, a slab or two cold, and sometimes raw, between
two thick slices of bread for "baggin'" or lunch, and
again, as often as not, for dinner (when the last of the
Sunday beef has been disposed of) cooked before the
fire, in a deep dish, and served up smoking and savoury
with "taters" in the gravy.   Here and there, when

5

you pass the more important dwelling of a "gradely farmer," you may smell Irish stew, or "toad in the hole," but bacon is the staple food of the cottagers, and they certainly seem to thrive on it. Look at this child

who suddenly comes toddling, spoon in hand, from the rear of this whitewashed cottage, and pauses irresolute at the sight of a stranger. "There's legs for you!" as Mrs. Poyser would say; and see the bare arms with their delicious roundness and little soft rings at the wrist, the chubby face, sunburnt over its clear red and white, all save the forehead which, as the yellow curls are tossed aside, shows snowy — or no! that is too lifeless a word to express it—rather warmly, delicately white, like the outer petals of a blush rose. Is not this a good advertisement for Thornleigh air and Thornleigh bacon? Presently the school-bell clangs out, and in a moment the hamlet is alive; no kiss of a fairy prince could dispel the very atmosphere of drowsiness so thoroughly and instantaneously as does the quavering jangling summons. Here be

" All the little boys and girls,
With rosy cheeks and flaxen curls,
And sparkling eyes and teeth like pearls,
Tripping and skipping. . . . ."

Truly, a hearty, healthy, merry little crew, these
Thornleigh children! Of all ages, from the mite above
described, who is scarcely two, to the stalwart urchin in
the Sixth Standard, whose wrists have crept such a
long way out of his jacket-sleeves, and whose feet in
their hob-nailed shoes make such a terrible clatter over
the cobble-stones. That is the boy who put a live eel
into the schoolmistress's letter-box one morning, nearly
causing that short-sighted and long-suffering person to
have a fit when she put in her hand in search of her
correspondence. Tommy was at once detected and
desired to hold *out* his hand, which he did, observing
philosophically that he might's well be hit for somethin'
as nothin'.

The little girls run past, dropping a hasty one-sided
" dip " as they recognise an acquaintance; their little
round rosy faces are still shining from their recent
scrub in the back kitchen—"the missus" is *that*
partickler—and the boys follow more slowly, for they
are whipping their tops as they go. Tops are in
fashion this summer, I perceive. There is a fashion in
village games which changes almost with the seasons;
last year the favourite playthings were miniature carts,

7

constructed very ingeniously out of old boxes, the wheels being made of disused cotton reels; and the year before they were still simpler, consisting merely of round pieces of tin—the lids of biscuit-boxes chiefly—with a hole in the middle, through which a long piece of string was passed. How gleefully the owners trundled and twirled them, and what a hideous din they made, and how unpleasant it was when one came whirling round you, entangling itself in your petticoats and rapping your shins!

There—the last of the boys has gone—a little brown-faced lad who rolls along with his hands in the pockets of his short corduroys, kicking up the dust as he walks, and shouting out contemptuous comments on the achievements of the top-whippers. Human nature is the same all over the world—I am inwardly convinced that this urchin is topless.

The children are no longer in sight, but I can hear them still, the boys shouting and cracking their whips, the girls playing in the road outside the school-house, for the bell has not yet stopped, and the last precious moments of liberty must be made the most of.

> *" Here we go round the mulberry bush,*
> *The mulberry bush, the mulberry bush,*
> *Here we go round the mulberry bush,*
> *This fine frosty morning."*

They shout the ditty in little breathless gusts; and even at this distance I can hear the shuffle of their dancing feet.

The bell is silent at last, and there is a general rush and scamper; then all is still.

Not for long, though. The hour of repose is over, and work begins again. There is a pushing back of chairs and benches, and a clatter of crockery within the houses, a tramp of heavy footsteps, a slouching past of burly forms without. Here comes Mr. Waring, one of the most important personages of Thornleigh; "a gradely farmer" as one can see at the first glance. All our farmers are fat, and the more prosperous they are, the fatter they grow.

His broad, shining, rubicund face wreathes itself in smiles as he approaches.

"Good arternoon, Mrs. Francis. Fine weather—ah, 'tis. We could do with a drop o' rain, though, to swell the potatoes." (Evidently Mr. Waring's hay is "carried.")

"It did rain a little this morning, didn't it?"

"Nobbut a spot or two, an' we'st ha' no moor while the wind's in yon quarter."

"Well, good day, Mr. Waring. I'm glad to have seen you. It's some time since we have met—I began to be afraid your gout was troubling you again."

"Nay, ma'am, I've kep' pretty clear o' that lately,

but it's been busy times with me. I've been gettin' th'
hay in, ye see, an' buryin' my father, an' that."

He touches his huge mushroom-shaped chip hat, and
rolls on, leaving me a little taken aback at the piece of
information thus casually conveyed. Not indeed that I
was surprised at the manner of the announcement, for
the Thornleigh folks are not as a rule given to sentiment,
but I *am* rather astonished to hear that Mr. Waring so
recently possessed a papa, he himself having been a
grandfather for some time.

A few steps more bring one out in the open fields
that stretch away, brown, and green, or rather golden
in the sunshine, to their boundary of distant sandhill.
The broad expanse has a certain beauty of its own in
spite of its flatness and monotony. On the right is a
half-cut meadow, the rich, heavily scented swathes
lying in the foreground, while a little further off the
mowing machine—a new one, brilliantly scarlet and
blue—flashes out against the young green of the wood,
the straw hat and bright-coloured shirt of the driver
adding to the picturesque effect. The sudden ejacula-
tion "Haw!" behind the hedge on my left makes me
start. The "turmits" are being earthed up, and a
stalwart labourer is in the act of turning his plough at
the end of a drill. His sunburnt face is uplifted for a
moment in greeting, the sleek sides of his elephantine
horse gleam through the green thorn-boughs; there is

a further bellow—"Gee-back!"—accompanied by an oath or two, merely used in the way of persuasion, and then up the furrow they go, patiently plodding.

The little village, as I look back at it, has suddenly become alive with rustic figures: men returning to work; women going in and out of their houses, the loose sleeves of their print jackets or "bedgowns" rolled up high on their arms, their short striped petti-coats leaving their sturdy ankles exposed to view. Chickens are being fed, pigs "done for"; then there is the washing-up and a thousand odd jobs to be seen to. The blue smoke curls up merrily: Farmer Waring was right, it will not rain to-day; here and there linen gleams out on hedges or clothes-lines, though most of the thrifty Thornleigh housewives have got their wash out of the way before this. These lines of white with the women's bedgowns and aprons, and the yellow corn-ricks, which seem positively to blaze in the sunlight, are vivid points of colour in a picture which is other-wise blended of sober hues. House walls, for the most part of time-worn stone, quarried from the "delf" yonder, roofs of thatch, or antique slabs of stone, lichen-grown, and irregularly set; here a cottage of brick, the red of which, however, is softened and mellowed by years, there one with walls washed over with ochre. Yonder stands the ivy-grown church placidly keeping watch over a goodly company of gravestones. This village churchyard is to my thinking the epitome of tranquillity and even beauty of a certain sober kind. It seems to me that the church casts its shadow lovingly across the graves, caressing each in

turn, for all who lie there have in life been gathered to its embrace many and many a time. Flowers bloom above the sleepers in abundance, old-fashioned and simple as themselves; for the village children make a garden of this place, and many a wreath of wild-flowers is woven by willing little fingers, many a fern and flowering bulb is eagerly, and often inefficiently, planted, to blossom, and wither, and be replaced. There is a special watering-pot kept in the school-porch which they call "the deading-can," because it is reserved for watering the graves. The fresh voices of the little ones mingle with the music of the birds in the neighbouring woods, the sweep of scythes, the clatter of reaping and mowing machines, the slow heavy tread of sleek farm-horses—all the thousand-and-one blithe sounds that gladden the heart of the rustic. One would think these "rude forefathers of the hamlet" must find it sweet to rest here, under the pure air of heaven, with the sun to shine on them, and the grasshoppers to chirp above them, and the little children to prattle near.

When I first knew Thornleigh "the Canon" was alive. He lies yonder now, under the green sod, on the spot where he so often stood to greet his parishioners as they entered or left the church.

No picture of the place would be complete without at least an outline of that familiar figure. Familiar indeed it was in Thornleigh; there was not a man, woman, or child in the place in whom he did not interest himself, and whose every idiosyncrasy was not known to him. The people considered it quite a matter of course that he should concern himself as much with their affairs as with his own. "Eh!" they would say among themselves, "Canon *will* be glad t'ear as our Bill's doin' so nicely," or "Canon 'll be fair broken-'earted when he gets to know Polly's goin's on." And it is only fair to say that these homely joys and sorrows were matters of the deepest moment to him. Nothing could be done in Thornleigh without the Canon's intervention. Sometimes he would be seen teaching a young mother how to hold and dandle her first baby, and sometimes assisting an inexperienced nurse in making a sick-bed; now looking in on old Billy Prescott the keeper (who was recovering painfully from his last spree), and recommending fearlessly " a hair of the dog that bit him " to the nervous miserable man—a prescription, be it said, which called forth a good deal of argument on the part of Billy's dame— and now sternly reprimanding a pair of youthful lovers whom he caught billing and cooing under a hedge when they should have been at Sunday-school. This " courtin' " or " company-keeping " was a sore point with the Canon, beginning, as it usually did, among lads and lasses who had only just left school, and being continued till they were quite old enough to know better. The Canon left no stone unturned in his efforts to combat the amative proclivities of his flock; when the boys and girls had outgrown that stage in which he could settle the matter by boxing their ears or complaining to their parents, or when there was no apparent reason for prolonging the wooing of more staid and well-to-do parties, or even when a match between a certain couple was considered "likely" by the neighbours, and advisable by himself, he was uncompromising and insistent in advocating matrimony. If "saucing," and remonstrating in private did not produce the desired result, he would throw out a hint or two on Sundays before the assembled congregation.

"It is quite time for that couple I met walking in the woods last night to be married," or, "If certain people who don't live a hundred miles away from here intend to be united before Lent, their banns must be called next Sunday."

And, strange to say, in all probability the couple in question were "shouted" on the appointed day. If they still hung back, the Canon generally let them know what he thought of them in the "few words" with which it was his custom to preface his ordinary Sunday discourse when any members of his congregation stood in special need of "pulling up." Those "few words" were terrible things, especially as the speaker used occasionally to detect people in the act of complacently "fitting the cap" on the guilty parties; whereupon he added another phrase or two to remind these censorious ones of *their* little weaknesses, ending not infrequently with a sweeping condemnation of Thornleigh and its ways in general. (Woe betide any one else, however, who ventured in his presence to say a word against Thornleigh, or Thornleigh folk!) The people liked him none the less for his occasional severity. "Eh, hasn't Canon been bargin' awful this mornin'?" they would ask of each other with a roll of the head, and a jerk of the thumb over the shoulder ; but on the whole they preferred being "barged at" to being let alone, on the same principle, presumably, as that which causes them and their kind to think nothing of a doctor who does not order nauseous draughts and bitter pills.

But if the Canon was zealous and unflinching in the performance of his duty, he knew how to temper justice with mercy. Many of the Thornleigh folk will wipe their eyes as they tell you of that cold winter's night, some years ago, when "poor owd Gillyf'er Jack" was sent by his crony the blacksmith to fetch home a quantity of old iron bolts and chains which the latter had bought at a recent sale. Poor Jack met a friend on the way, and they had "an odd gill" (a *very* odd gill) together, after which the friend went his way and Jack went his—which in some unaccountable manner led him into a ditch. There the Canon found him, half suffocated and but partially sober, and after much difficulty extricated him and set him on his legs. But perceiving that Jack was only just capable of carrying himself, and could in no way have proceeded if encumbered with his burden, the Canon took up the load himself. Off they set, the Canon staggering and gasping for breath, and Jack staggering too, and occasionally lurching against his companion so violently that the chains jingled again; and at other times making such a swerve in the other direction that the Canon thought he was going to take "a header" into the ditch once more. In his anxiety he shifted his load to one shoulder, and passing the other arm through Jack's so as to enable him to maintain his equilibrium in some degree, they proceeded onwards in a curious zig-zag fashion until they came to the village. Here the Canon was for taking leave of his protégé, but Jack having now reached the affectionate stage of intoxication, refused to part with him until he had seen *him* safe home. He poured forth, indeed, so many loving, if somewhat indistinct, remonstrances in so loud a key that presently the whole village assembled, anxious to see " what mak' o' drunken chap Jack o' Gillyf'er's had gotten howd of?" And much surprised they were to find their own pastor in Jack's tipsy embrace, blushing with discomfiture, and sorely exhausted by his evening's work.

Gillyf'er Jack was not the only member of the congregation who was anxious to act as escort on occasion to the good priest. His cousin Joe Rutherford (Ned's Joe) used to consider it his special privilege to " see Canon home o' nights." If the latter were returning by train from some distant expedition he would be sure to find Joe waiting for him at the station, and the

17   B

servants at the Hall, or any of the neighbouring houses where he occasionally dined, were quite accustomed to Joe's vigorous thump at the back-door, and the subsequent announcement that he had " coom for Canon."

It was, however, the sick and infirm of his flock who made the largest demands on the Canon's time; he would prescribe for them, and comfort them; listen to long accounts of their symptoms, inspect their "bad legs," and compassionate their sore fingers with untiring patience and kindness. Then, as to his spiritual ministrations, the persevering exhortations to some, the quiet "word in season" to another, the mere comfort of his presence in a death-chamber—where he would kneel for hours by the poor bed-side, clasping the inert hands in his, while the fast-glazing eyes were turned towards him until they could see no more—one should hear the Thornleigh folk tell of these things. A poor girl lay dying of consumption once in the village—a farm servant and a stranger; there was no one belonging to her to attend her, or to mourn for her, and her mistress, though she " did for her " with a certain rough kindness, was too busy to be much comfort to her. The Canon therefore considered it incumbent on him to spend many hours of each day with her. Towards the end of her illness, it was the poor creature's one joy to hear him pray beside her. The Lord's Prayer pleased her best, and to gratify her he repeated it dozens and dozens of times. Sometimes when she lay absolutely still with closed eyes, he would fancy that the monotonous sound had sent her to sleep, and try to creep away unperceived, but she would stretch out a feeble

hand and whisper a request for "one more 'Our Father.'" And then the Canon would kneel and begin again a very litany, until his voice was broken with fatigue and his dry tongue clove to his palate. "Who knows, I might want a prayer myself when I am dying," he said, when some one remonstrated with him. She passed away at last and was forgotten, and it was not

until the Canon's own last illness came that this circum-
stance was recalled to the mind of his people. For
when it became patent that their beloved friend and
master was to be taken from them, the children knelt
by scores about his door and in the adjoining church,
and their elders joined them by relays, and prayed from
morning till the late summer dusk. All day long the
sound of children's voices was wafted in through the
open window of the room where the Canon lay preparing for his great journey, and curiously enough, the
prayer chosen by the little ones, the music of which
accompanied him to the very threshold of Eternity, was
the "Our Father."

GAFFER'S CHILD

GAFFER'S
CHILD

ABOUT half a mile from the village proper is a certain neat white cottage standing in its own potato plot, and surrounded by fields. This was inhabited for many years by an old couple, their only daughter, and an elderly labourer, a lodger, whose small but regular weekly payments eked out their tiny income. The father and mother, Middleton by name, shortened for convenience sake into the less aristocratic but more suggestive title of "Midden," were both deprived of the use of their limbs, and passed the greater part of their lives in large elbow-chairs on either side of the fireplace. After Betsy their daughter had washed and dressed them of a morning, she and the lodger "shifted" them from the bed with its blue checked curtains to these ; and then the lodger straightened his back and nodded at them, and "reckoned they'd do," and went off to his work. And Betsy, when she had finished her scrubbing and cleaning up in the house, betook herself to the garden; and all day long the old pair sat and stared at each other from opposite sides of the hearth, for the most part in silence, though sometimes they compared ailments, and sometimes they had a little quarrel.

One day Tom Middleton died; and then there was only one old body to wash and dress, and seat by the fire.

When they carried her out of her room as usual, the first morning after her husband's funeral, Mrs. Midden turned her head and looked about her.

" What's gettin' Feyther's cheer ? "

" It's yonder, aside of the dresser," answered Betsy, growing suddenly a little pink about the eyes.

" Then fetch it out, an' set it wheer it allus was."

So the empty chair was placed in its former place, and the old woman sat and looked at it, day after day, till one morning she too was " shifted " for the last time, and Betsy put both chairs against the wall.

Poor Betsy was alone in the world now, and cried a great deal in consequence, and sat for hours with her apron over her head; but presently she began to recover herself, and to take comfort in the thought that as it *was* to be it had happened before her " blacks " were worn out.

"If it had but ha' been the Lord's will to ha' took her at the same time as Feyther, we needn't have had but the one buryin'," she remarked with a sob.

"Ah," said Ned Gill, the lodger, "but ye see things never falls out the way we'st ha' them if we'd aught to say to them. And the Almighty no doubt knows best. It might ha' comed more expensive i' the long run."

"Eh, that's true," assented Betsy, and then she gave honest Ned his dinner in a handkerchief, and told him he'd best be trotting.

Betsy at this time was about forty-two; short, stout, and hard-featured enough, though she had very kindly blue eyes, and a bright good-humoured smile. She and Neddy Gill were excellent friends, and neither of them saw any reason why she should not continue to "do for" him now as she had for the last ten years. She was therefore considerably startled and annoyed when one morning the Canon, alarmed for the proprieties, suggested that under existing circumstances it would be as well for her to look out for another lodger.

"What for?" said Betsy, pausing with her foot on the spade—she had been earthing up her potatoes—and looking round with a puzzled face.

"Well, you see, Betsy, you're a single woman, and living quite alone—it's not (ahem!) quite nice to have a man lodging here. You'd better try to find a woman or a married couple to stay with you if you must let lodgings. It would be much pleasanter for you too. You would have company all day long, you know."

"I dunnot want no more company nor what I have," returned Betsy, stolidly. "I couldn't be moidered wi' folks in the house i' th' daytime, an' I couldn't do with women at all. I've my work to do inside an' out, an' no time for aught else. An' arter Ned takes his breakfast i' th' morning he's out o' th' road all day, an' of an evenin' I've got used to see him sittin' in a corner smokin's pipe."

Here Betsy spat in her hands and turned over another shovelful of earth.

"Well, but, Betsy——"

"Ah, I've got used to Neddy, you see, an' I reckon he's used to me," she interrupted, glancing up again. "We's do very well, Canon, thank ye."

"Well, Betsy—in that case—don't you think you and Ned had better be married?"

Betsy plied her spade with great vigour, and made no answer.

"You see," urged the Canon, "you really might just .as well. It would make very little difference to either of you, and would stop people from talking. Besides, it would be nice for you to feel you were no longer alone in the world, and to have some one to take care of you, and work for you."

Betsy drove her spade slowly into the ground, and rested her foot on it once more.

"Ah," she said calmly, "that's true enough. I never thought o' that before. Well, Canon, I reckon you'd best speak to Ned. I haven't got no objections."

The Canon withdrew, in some amusement, and Betsy went on with her work. An hour or two later Ned's well-known slow step was heard on the path, but instead of proceeding straight to the house as he usually did when he returned of an evening, he went up to her and stood beside her.

"Have ye seen Canon?" inquired Betsy, without looking up.

"Ah," returned Ned.

"Well?" said Betsy.

"Well—I've nought agin it."

"Ah—well—neither have I. It'll not make such a deal of difference, neither, as Canon says."

Ned stood for a moment or two contemplating the sturdy figure of his future helpmate with a queer half-puzzled smile on his weather-beaten face; then he observed that he had told Canon he might as well shout them next Sunday.

"Ye did, did ye?" returned Betsy. "Sounds like business, that."

She suddenly straightened herself, and handed Neddy the spade with an engaging smile.

27

"Sin' that's how it's to be," she observed, "ye might's well finish the taters."

A happier couple than Betsy and Neddy—"Gaffer," as she called him—it would be hard to find. There was but one drawback to their bliss—theirs was the fate of the proverbial king and queen in the old fairy tales; they had no children. This was, perhaps, scarcely to be surprised at, a fact which Betsy frequently endeavoured to impress on her spouse.

"Wheer do ye suppose we's find childer at our time o' life?" she would ask him a little impatiently. "Ye sh'd ha' wed before, if ye'd wanted that mak' o' work."

"Ah, that's true enough, lass," Gaffer would reply; "but eh—I'd be proud if we was t' ave a little un of our own. A pretty little thing wi' rosy cheeks as 'ud come runnin' t' th' gate when I'd be comin' whoam of an evenin'."

"Eh, ye're nobbut an owd foo'," Betsy would say, in rather shaky tones though. "A pretty un, too! It's likely, I'm sure? Why didn't ye think o' that before, an' tak' up wi' some gradely young lass twenty or thirty year ago? Ye'd ha' had childer enough by this, I'll uphowd ye."

"Ah, happen I would," Ned would assent; "an' yet, missus, I doubt if any young lass 'ud do for me an' that same way as you. I've nought again you at all, missus. Nay, nought any way.. I've bin—I've bin as comfortable

as I'd iver ax to be—so theer! Retch me the 'bacco—
we'st say no more about it."

Betsy felt that this was very handsome on Ned's part;
and his tolerance made her regret more than ever her
inability to gratify him on the particular point in
question. She allowed her husband henceforth various
small latitudes against which she had hitherto set her
face; such as the keeping of a dog, though that, as she
frequently observed, was a mak' o' cratur she never could
abide. She also permitted him to fill the house with
neighbours' children as often as he fancied, enduring
good-humouredly enough, the noise they made, and the
" strew " and general disorder in her tidy kitchen. In
time, indeed, she herself grew fond of their little visitors,
and sometimes when she saw her Gaffer with a flaxen-
haired mite on his knee, or prepared a " jam-butty " for
some small petitioner whose chubby hands clung to her
skirts, and whose laughing eyes were raised roguishly to
hers, honest Betsy would heave a deep sigh of regretful
longing.

It is not very often that in such cases as this, a
demand creates a supply; indeed, as a young Irish
friend remarked in my hearing once, " It is always the
best mothers who have no children; " but, curiously
enough, the intense wish of the good couple was
gratified after many years in quite an unexpected
manner.

It happened that in a certain country town five or six miles from Thornleigh a little stranger made its appearance, finding no welcome ready for it, and indeed being considered very much in the way.

The father had emigrated and was not to be heard of; the mother a servant, and a simple foolish young thing, was far from home and kindred. It would have fared badly with her had she been cast adrift; but her mistress, who was much attached to her, consented to keep her if the baby could be satisfactorily disposed of. This charitable lady therefore consulted a friend of hers, who consulted the Canon, who consulted Mrs. Gill, who consulted Ned; and the result was general jubilation.

"It'll be Gaffer's child," said Betsy. "I left it to him to settle, and he's all for takin' it. But the only fear is, Canon, if the mother goes and takes it from us just as we're gettin' fond on it, it'll go near to break's heart."

"I don't think you need fear that," said the Canon. "The poor creature is only too thankful to get rid of it, and her mistress promises to see that she pays for its keep regularly."

"Eh, well, that'll be a very good job too. I dunnot say as the money won't come in," responded thrifty Betsy. And so the matter was settled.

The day before the baby took up its abode with its

foster parents, Gaffer Ned walked up to Thornleigh
Hall, and after a little preliminary beating about the
bush, inquired, with a bashful grin, if there mightn't be
such a thing as an owd cradle of some mak' or other to
be bestowed for the asking. Well, there *was* a cradle
which the last occupant had outgrown and of which she
had taken possession for her dolls; but with a little
persuasion she was induced to part with it; sheets,
blankets, and counterpane were hunted up, and it was
presented to Ned. To see his face when the be-frilled
and be-ribboned "bassinette" was
brought down! His eyes positively shone with rapture, and
his mouth pursed itself up
into a comical expression
of admiring satisfaction.
Then the reverence with
which he took hold of it,
the care with which he
carried it, almost as
though already a baby
face lay on the lace-
trimmed pillow! His
way lay 'through the
village, and as he marched along with his burden a good
many sly jokes were made at his expense. But brave
old Neddy held on his way stoutly and good-humouredly,

turning his jolly wrinkled face over his shoulder now and then to respond to some neighbour's sally, or to utter a witticism of his own: he was so happy, he was as ready to laugh as any of them.

. Next day Betsy donned her best garments and went to fetch the baby, which was delivered over to her by its temporary nurse with much satisfaction. Gaffer went to meet her as she returned, and insisted on taking possession of the child, while his wife trudged joyfully beside him, carrying its little wardrobe and its bottle. When they got in-doors, Ned sat down carefully, and with big, eager, trembling fingers unfolded the little one's wraps, gazing for some moments in silence at the placid face.

"Missus, come here," he whispered presently to Betsy, who was "taking off her things" at the other side of the room.

She drew near, smiling. The infant's tiny hands clasped Gaffer's great horny forefinger.

"Eh, owd lass, th' A'mighty's good!" said Ned, "we'n got a little un o' we're own at last."

It was pleasant to see Betsy assume the airs and importance of a materfamilias of long standing. To see her dandle the infant, and pat it on the back, and administer "cinder-tea" on occasion; and to hear her discuss with other matrons its ailments: the teeth which according to her it began to "breed" at the age of about six weeks, the "notice" which it already took, and various other points of equally absorbing interest. All this was pleasant enough, but it was still more delight- ful to see "Gaffer" with the child.

He got up half an hour earlier in the morning that he might have time to assist at its toilet before going to his work, and would stand watching its ab- lutions with intense interest, his face wrinkled up into the funniest mixture of pride and anxiety.

"Dunnot she come on wonderful?" Betsy would say, sustaining the pink morsel in the basin with one hand over which the helpless little head drooped and bobbed in the effort to sustain itself.

"She do, bless her little 'eart!" Neddy would answer, with modest triumph.

One day the baby crowed and kicked in the water for the first time, and the old couple fell a-laughing until they were obliged to wipe the tears of ecstasy from their eyes. And sometimes she cried, and then Ned sternly reprimanded Betsy, and wanted to know what she was about to let the poor child break its 'eart like that without doing something for it.

He would hurry home in the evening, putting away his tools with all speed, and polishing his hands on the legs of his trousers.

"Now missus," he would call out. "Hand over."

And Betsy, nothing loth, "handed over" the child; to be cuddled and dandled and sung to—"at least," as she sometimes explained to her neighbours, "Gaffer doesn't exactly sing, for he can't, but he makes a kind of noise—an' he's pleased, an' she's pleased—an' so all's reet."

Meanwhile the child grew and throve amazingly; the weekly pension was paid regularly, but the mother never once came to see her.

"Onnatural I call it," observed Betsy, and then with a sigh half jealous, half relieved, "well—happen it's all for th' best."

Just as little Polly was nine months old, and had begun to lisp "Da-da," and to spring and wriggle in Betsy's arms when she heard Ned's step, news came to the white cottage which plunged its inhabitants in desolation. Polly's mother had got into bad ways, and her mistress said she could no longer keep her, and she was bent on going to London, and, worse than all, on taking Baby Polly with her.

" I knowed how it 'ud be," sobbed Betsy.

" Didn't I tell 'ee ? " murmured Gaffer in a choked voice ; and after a pause, turning to the woman—a friend of Polly's mother—who had been sent to make the announcement and to fetch the child, " Nay, but ye might tell her, as we dunnot hold to the bit o' money comin' reg'lar, if it's that as she's got in her head—we'd be fain to keep the little un for nought. Tell her that, and tell her as she needn't fear but it'll be well done to —an'—an'—" with a sob, " the missus an' me will be fair heart-broken to part with it."

The friend was quite sure of that, and very sorry, but it couldn't be helped. The mother wanted her child, and she had promised to fetch it ; so if Mrs. Gill wouldn't mind putting its bits of things together she'd like to be going.

Mrs. Gill, after many expostulations and reproaches, was obliged to comply, and at last the bundle was tied up, and the baby received tearful farewell embraces from her foster-parents. But events proved that they had counted without this baby: she had submitted placidly enough to be bonneted and cloaked and wept over ; but when it came to be handed over to a strange woman and carried down the road, leaving Dada and Mammie standing by the gate, it was quite another matter. Polly displayed an energy and determination which no one had hitherto given her credit for. She screamed, she kicked, she fought " like a little soldier," as Betsy subsequently remarked with great pride, she doubled herself up and turned black in the face, and finally when everything else failed prepared to go into convulsions. When it came to this her new acquaintance hurried back and almost flung her into Betsy's arms.

"Take her, for God's sake," she cried. " I'll have no more to do with her. She'd be dead before I carried her half-way. If her mother wants her, let her come and fetch her herself."

But the mother did not come; whether her friend's account of the Gills' unwillingness to part with Polly, and Polly's unwillingness to part with them, had touched or frightened her, did not transpire; but the honest couple were after this left in undisturbed possession of their treasure. The fact that from that day forward they never received a penny for its keep rather increased than diminished their satisfaction.

Two years passed very uneventfully, and Polly had become one of the prettiest children in the neighbourhood of Thornleigh. Many of the neighbours shook their heads over the idolatrous worship of the honest couple for their little prattling, sunny-headed nursling.

"I niver did hold wi' sp'ilin' childer that gate," one wise matron would observe to another. " Ned's fair silly about you, an' Betsy's nigh as bad. An' when ye come to think, ye know, what it is, an' wheer it's comed from."

"Yigh," the other would respond, "I 'ope they mayn't be layin' up disapp'intment for theirsel's. I doubt it'll not come to much good—no more nor its mother. There's allus a deal o' trouble wi' childer o' that mak' as didn't ought to live at all."

No baby princess, however, could have been considered of more importance, or in her own way more tenderly nurtured than this poor little waif that "didn't ought to ha' lived at all." And when she said her prayers at Betsy's knee, or slept with smiling lips and chubby folded hands, she really looked quite as good and innocent as a child need be. It was wonderful, the neighbours said.

One warm Sunday afternoon Ned was sitting in the doorway smoking his pipe, Betsy being established a little farther within the house, spelling out *The Weekly Mercury* which was her staple Sunday literature. Polly was taking a little nap in an impromptu bed composed of the two arm-chairs once used by Betsy's parents. A Sabbath stillness was reigning everywhere; all the church-goers and lovers and Sunday-school children were "out o' the road"; and the silence was only broken by the trill of a lark circling downwards just within the range of Ned's vision, and the hum of bees.

Ned followed the motions of the lark with tranquil enjoyment, puffing luxuriously at his pipe the while; and when the bird's song suddenly ceased, as, after completing its final circle, it darted to earth, his eyes, descending also, encountered those of a stranger standing by his gate. Dark eyes they were, weary and anxious-looking, yet with a latent fierceness in them which somehow startled Ned. But when the girl spoke, it was in a gentle and timid voice.

"Would ye kindly give me a drink of water? I—have walked a long way and am tired."

"Ah, come in, do, an' rest ye a bit," responded Ned, removing the pipe from his mouth. "We mun find ye summat better than water though. The missus 'll be gettin' the tay in a two-three minutes. Come in, an' sit ye down."

The girl opened the gate and entered, dragging her feet in their dusty, ill-made boots—the high heels of which had been worn quite crooked—in a way which

38

betokened extreme fatigue. Her crimson skirt was draggled and covered with dust, and her dark hair, though dressed in the height of the fashion, was rough and untidy.

Betsy eyed her with some disfavour, and reckoned she'd best set her a chair nigh the door where 't'ud be cooler; but the strange girl stepped past her into the little kitchen and peered about curiously.

"It's a snug little place," she said; "d'ye live here all alone—you two?"

Betsy was at first disposed to be offended at the freedom of the question, but her heart softened as she glanced at the visitor. She was nobbut a slip of a lass after all who knew no better. Poor thing, she *did* look pale too, and tired—her eyes were quite wild.

"All alone," echoed Betsy drearily, "nobbut the child."

"The child?"

"Ah, theer she lays yonder. Nay, see, she's wakkened up."

At this moment, in truth, a little ruffled flaxen head reared itself over the back of one of the chairs, and a drowsy voice called "Mammie."

The visitor stood as if turned to stone, but no stone was ever of such a hue as suddenly overspread those cheeks of hers: if they had been white before they were red enough now.

39

"Eh, my pretty lamb!" cried Betsy, who at this moment had no eyes for anything but the child, "come then, come wakken up an' show thy bonny face."

Polly, who had been vigorously rubbing her eyes with her chubby little fists, held out her arms now with a sleepy smile, blinked a great deal, and made some rather incoherent remark in tones still husky from her recent slumber.

"Now, then," said Betsy, brimming over with motherly pride, "come an' say 'Good arternoon,' pretty—theer's a good little lass." She carried her over to the visitor who turned with what seemed a little effort and looked at the child fixedly.

"She is a bonny little thing," she said, and paused. "She has got blue eyes, I see," she continued, adding with a sort of defiant glance at her hostess; "I always notice eyes first."

"Nay, but look ye here," cried Betsy, offended as the other moved a little away, without admiring half Polly's "points"; "see her legs—and these here little arms, as mottled—an' as firm. Feel of them."

The girl clasped them for a moment and then loosed her hold, colouring again all over her face.

"I can't bear to look at her," she said. "I had a—sister with blue eyes once."

"Ah, an' she's dead, I reckon," said Betsy, commiseratingly.

"Yes, long since. There is no one belonging to me now."

"Well, sit ye down, an' we'll have tay directly. Run to Dada, Polly."

Polly toddled off on her little unsteady legs, shouting as Ned caught her up in his arms to kiss and tickle her.

"You look old folk to have such a young child?" said the visitor suddenly.

"Ah, more like her grandfeyther and grandma I doubt," said Betsy with a jolly laugh. "But she isn't our child, you see, raly, though yet in a way she is."

"How's that?"

Betsy, nothing loth to tell a tale in which she took never-failing delight, recounted Polly's history while she bustled about preparing for tea; dwelling especially on the little un's amazing cleverness in declining to return to her unnatural parent.

"When I tell ye that she was living for nine months within a few miles o' the child, an' niver come next or nigh her. A nice life of it the poor lamb 'ud have had with her."

"Perhaps," said the girl absently, for she was watching the little leaping crowing figure in Gaffer's arms, "perhaps the poor creature was ashamed."

"Pooh," cried Betsy, setting her arms akimbo, and looking as if she could say something very sarcastic if

41

she chose, "ashamed, indeed! Here, Gaffer, come to your tay."

Gaffer came in, carrying Polly, whom he seated on his knee, and regaled with a drink out of his saucer, the tea having been previously cooled with much blow-- ing.

"Well, whichever way it is, I'm reet thankful to keep the little un," resumed Betsy, when she had attended to the wants of her guest. "Gaffer an' me wouldn't know what to do wi' ourselves without her."

"The mother might turn up some day yet and want her back though," said the stranger, stooping to pick up her spoon which she had dropped.

"Nay," said Gaffer. I dunnot think she will. I raly dunnot. We'n never had a word nor a line for two year very near. An' if she did come back——"

"Ah, if she did!"

"Well, then, the missus an' me has it settled between us to mak' out a terrible bill for the keep o' the child. Ye see we'n niver had a penny sin' she was nine month old—an' we'll mak' out such a bill for food, an' clothes, an' our trouble, ye know, wi' minding her, as she'll niver be able to pay. So then we'll say as we mun keep th' child till she does."

Here Gaffer winked across the table at his missus, and leant back in his chair chuckling at his own foresight and sagacity.

42

"That's our plan, ye see," he added, bending down to poke a little bit of tea-cake into Polly's expectant mouth.

"Is that your plan?" said the stranger, looking full at him. "Well, it may be a good one for you, but I think it's cruel hard on the mother. The child's hers after all, and no matter how low she may have fallen, she has the best right to it. The very beasts love their young ones, ye know."

"Well, but see now," said Gaffer earnestly. "Look at this child; would ye ever wish to see a healthier or a bonnier one? An' 'ark to her sayin' her little prayers an' hymns an' that—eh, the missus have brought her up wonderful. We reckon to do th' best for her as ever we can. She'll have her schoolin' an' be taught her religion, and when she gets a big lass an' is happen thinkin' o' gettin' wed we's find her a bit o' brass to help her set up house. She s'all be good an' 'appy if we can mak' her so, you may depend on that. An' if her mother goes an' takes her off us, what'll she do wi' her, think you? I've nought agin her, poor soul, and I wish she may come to no harm" (Gaffer said this in a tone which implied that he thought it extremely likely that she would), "but arter all she is but a foolish bit of a thing as couldn't keep straight when she 'ad the chance given her. What sort of trainin' would she give the poor child? It's well if she didn't make her just such another as hersel'. Nay, nay, we're i' th' reet to keep the poor innocent from her if we can."

The girl did not answer; her eyes were cast down, and there was a curious look on her face.

"Now, Polly," said Ned, "let's hear ye say grace. Eh, she does say it so nice. 'Ark to 'er now."

Polly's two little hands were somewhat forcibly joined, and she lisped out an infantile version of a "grace after meat," with many gasps and stops, and not a few promptings, her blue eyes roving round the table the while. Ned beamed with pride and triumph, and was loth to allow the performance to end even with the "Amen."

"Let's ha' th' neet prayers now. Ye'll niver believe" (in a rapturous aside) "how wonderful she says 'em."

Polly, drawing a very long breath, started off at a brisk canter through the "Our Father," adding eagerly and impatiently "God b'ess dada and mammie—God b'ess me an' make me a good 'ittle lass—dat's all."

Was that indeed all?

"Does she never say a prayer for her mother?" cried the girl, speaking in a strange harsh voice and rising from her chair. "I mean her own mother. D'ye never make her pray for her?"

"Well, ye see," returned Betsy, "we'n got to look on her as our own, I may say. I reckon we didn't make much count o' th' mother, poor creatur', an' happen when all's said an' done, it's best not to be namin' her to the innocent child."

"Oh, you are hard folks!" exclaimed the stranger passionately, "you are cruel folks! Oh, my God, it's a hard, cruel world! Ye might, ye might have let the child pray."

She stopped, choked with sobs, and, suddenly snatching Polly from Ned's arms, kissed her fiercely and rushed out of the house.

As soon as the good couple had in some measure recovered from their astonishment, they rushed to the door, but the shabby figure was already out of sight.

"Eh, what mak' of wench is yon?" cried Betsy, gazing at her husband in great perturbation. "Eh, poor misfort'nate thing, I reckon she's in trouble. I misdoubt me sore she's not much good, poor creatur'. Happen she an' our Polly's mother is a pair."

"Nay, missus," groaned Gaffer. "I doubt they're wan. We'n been a pair of fools, missus, that's what it is. Yon poor lass is our Polly's mother hersel'."

"But she's left the child," stammered Betsy after a pause, "for good."

Yes, she had left the child—for good.

CELEBRITIES

A VILLAGE community is much like any other community "when all's said and done" (to use a phrase common in Thornleigh). Births and weddings, illnesses and deaths, partings and home-comings, take place at rarer intervals, no doubt, than in more populous places, and everybody knows everything about everybody else (and sometimes a good deal more than there is to know); but after all the broad lines of life are the same in a village as elsewhere, and human nature is human nature all the world over. Thornleigh, quiet and easy-going as it is, is not altogether behind the age either; indeed its tiny stage has been the scene of many curious dramas, and it has numbered among its inhabitants some that would be notabilities anywhere.

Not so long ago there was a saint in Thornleigh—a genuine saint, called Peter Murphy. As his name betokens, he was an Irishman, though he had lived in the village long enough to be no longer looked on as an interloper. A tall emaciated old man, with long grey hair and very blue eyes, and a drop at the end of his nose, at all times and in all weathers, which was called by the irreverent "holy water." He had "revelations,"

and "spiritual consolations," and wrestlings with the Evil One, and always carried a large bone rosary, which he would lovingly finger during every spare moment he could snatch from his work. Once when Peter was ill the rosary disappeared, a fact which he announced with mingled ire and triumph. Some one weakly suggested that the old woman who "did for him" might have hidden it somewhere in dusting and tidying, but he dismissed the notion with scorn.

"Not at all," he said, "not—at—*all*. It's th' owld boy. I know that very well"—jerking his thumb over his shoulder with an unpleasantly significant gesture —"but I'm up to his thricks. Ha! I'll be even with him—*I'll* settle him!"

The methods which Peter made use of in the conflict never transpired, but that he ultimately came off victorious was demonstrated by the reappearance of "the bades," which thenceforth he wore for greater security round his neck.

His chief delight was to beguile the Canon into a theological discussion, and it was fine to hear him laying down the law, putting forward one abstruse thesis after another, and generally crushing his adversary with a reference to "Pope Celestinus," whose authority he considered conclusive.

Once, and only once, did Peter's holy calm desert him, and that was during certain elections which took place when Home Rule first began to be the question of the hour. All poor old Peter's national instincts asserted themselves, and he became as wildly excited as the most enthusiastic Parnellite of the present day. He even fell foul of his "clargy" whose political views did not coincide with his own, and meeting the priest one day accused him sternly of "voting for Herod," an outburst of which he subsequently repented, acknowledging in bitterness of spirit that the election was a "snare."

The village poetess is of the same nationality as Peter, and shares his political views and his partiality for fine words. She "disposes" her shawl about her shoulders, she "prostrates" on her bed; but it is when the mood for versifying seizes her that she shows of what she is really capable.

Her genius chiefly displays itself in the composition of dirges, one of which goes the round of the village after any melancholy event; and once she was inspired to write a plea for the Disestablishment of the Church of England. A terrible paper this, abounding in exhortations to "gory tyrants," and in references to "clanking chains."

It is a thing to remember when the authoress recites one of these masterpieces, swaying her body to and fro and making sweeping gestures, her eye meanwhile "in fine frenzy rolling," and her voice growing louder and more impassioned as she warms to her subject. I can only recall two consecutive lines, however, of one effusion, a lament on the death of her beloved priest, in which regret for his loss was mingled with anxiety as to his successor.

> "*Let not his lordship, the bishop, think with him I mean to interfair,*
> *But I hope he'll appoint an Irishman to his evacuated chair.*"

Apropos of frenzy, we had a real madman in Thornleigh once. We knew he had been "off" it" for a good bit, for his wife used occasionally to lock up his hat and boots to prevent his going out, and was not infrequently seen pelting him with mud in the village street "o' nights," as a gentle means of persuading him to

come home to bed. But nobody heeded poor Joe's
vagaries, and Thornleigh was considerably startled
when one morning the news flew from house to house
that he was raving mad. There had been sports in the
squire's park on the preceding day, in
honour of the Queen's jubilee, at which
every man, woman, and child in the place
had assisted, even the village Radical, who
was wont to relate to an awestricken and
incredulous audience how once he
had walked all the way to Liverpool to see her Majesty, and how
after all when he had got there
he'd seen "nought but a woman in
black." Well, poor Joe had taken
part in a tug of war, and woke up
next morning under the impression that it was entirely
owing to his exertions that Thornleigh had gained the
day. He spent the whole forenoon walking round and
round in a small circle in front of "The Hall," pausing
occasionally to tug at the bell and claim his prize.
Five pounds was the reward to which he considered
himself entitled, and failing that he had apparently
made up his mind to gyrate on that particular spot
for an indefinite period. Persuasions were tried, then
threats; various small offerings were put forth to tempt
him; finally the squire himself came out to reason with

him, but Joe, still twirling round and round in the
broiling sun, remained obdurate; five pounds were his
deserts, and five pounds he meant to have. But he
wouldn't mind, he observed with an insinuating leer,
when the aforesaid teetotum-performance next brought
him face to face with the squire, he wouldn't mind
treatin' the young ladies to the theayter with some of
it, he wouldn't mind *that* at all; he would take them
himself, an' the squire might come too if he liked. In
desperation the butler had recourse to strategy, and
walking up to Joe managed to break the magic circle,
slipping his arm through his and marching him off
homewards, pouring some apparently intensely confi-
dential communication into the lunatic's ears as he
went. Presently he returned jubilant, with the announcement that Joe was tucked up in bed quite
comfortable, and expecting the five-pound note to
arrive by post. He wouldn't get out again, he added,
as the womankind had taken away his clothes and
locked him into the room. But Joe was not to be
stopped by such slight obstacles as these; he broke
open the door as if it had been made of pasteboard,
and announced his intention of proceeding to the Hall
forthwith in his shirt. His garments being conse-
quently restored to him, he made quite a triumphant
progress through the village and enjoyed himself
amazingly; knocking down his papa to begin with—

making nothing of the latter's seventeen stone—then " chivying " his aunt till she was obliged to take refuge in the barn and to defend herself with a pitchfork, and finally betaking himself to the Hall where he played " peep-bo " with the stable-men, sent the gardeners spinning when they endeavoured to lay hands on him, broke open a few doors, and laid about him right and left with a stout staff, all in the most light-hearted and affable manner possible. At last one of the keepers had the happy inspiration of firing blank cartridges over his head, whereupon Joe took to his heels and fled like a hare, never stopping indeed till he reached his own home, and crept under the table. He was ultimately secured with stout cords, and his father sat opposite to him, cracking a horsewhip now and then by way of soothing him, until the police came to end poor Joe's frolic by carrying him off to the county asylum.

Some years ago a lad was attending Thornleigh school who promised to render his native village celebrated in more ways than one. A black-eyed, rosy-cheeked, rough-looking boy, with nevertheless a fine artistic perception, and a perfect passion for drawing. Had that boy been given facilities for cultivating it there is no saying what he might not have done, but as it was—well, I must tell his story.

His name was Johnnie Birch—Johnnie o' John's he

was usually called, to distinguish him from various kins-
folk of the same name—and his father was a small
farmer with a large family, who looked forward eagerly
to the time when his eldest son should be of age to help
him in field work and thus save " hire." Johnnie's
schooling was in itself a trial; indeed, Mr. Birch had
gone so far as to interview the mistress on the subject.

" Can't 'ee run him through them standards a bit
faster ? I'd be willin' to pay double the fee if ye'd
get him through two at a time ? Come, now—is that a
bargain ? "

But it wasn't. The schoolmistress assured him it
couldn't be done, and John Birch (John o' Joe's) retired
grumbling more against " book larnin'" than ever. If
the time which his son perforce employed in such
matters was held by him to be wasted, one may readily
infer with what patience he viewed Johnnie's growing
devotion to the fine arts.

"If I catch ye at any more o' that gammon!" the
elder John would say, driving home the lesson with a
box on the ears; and Johnnie junior would jump up in
a great hurry and hide away his papers. He could
better endure to have his ears boxed than to see his
beloved drawings torn up or burnt. In spite of the
parental disapproval he continued to draw, or to attempt
to draw, everything which he saw. The Canon chancing
to see some of his performances was struck with their

56

cleverness, and being himself no mean artist offered to give him some lessons. John o' Joe's consent was withheld for a long time, and at last only given on the understanding that as soon as his son had left school all that nonsense must cease.

Meanwhile Johnnie made the very best use of his time and astonished his master by his progress. The latter, not content with verbal instruction, lent him books and drawings to study at home; and bestowed on him, moreover, a sheaf of old Art Papers to peruse at his leisure. Some of these contained lives of various great artists, and Johnnie's eyes grew round, and his face flushed, as he read how many of them were poor boys like himself, and began by scratching their drawings on stones, or decorating garret walls with burnt stick. The moral was obvious: Johnnie too drew on stones with the point of his knife, and on whitewashed walls with charcoal of his own manufacture—why should not *he* be a celebrated painter? It was very hard after this to be called upon to feed the pigs, or to clean out the shippons. Day by day he set about these tasks with more unwillingness, and day by day his father grew more displeased. As his fourteenth birthday drew near, Johnnie's uneasiness increased; though he had by no means passed all the standards (for his artistic studies somewhat lessened his zeal for the acquirement of ordinary knowledge), his father would then be free to

keep him at home, his drawing lessons would cease, and he must make up his mind to lead thenceforth the life of an ordinary labourer. The boy fretted and fumed, and at·last, his very desperation giving

him courage,
betook himself
to Thornleigh Hall
to petition the Squire
himself to intercede for him. If the Squire would ask his father to let him be an artist, Johnnie thought

he would not refuse. He took with him five or six of his very finest works of art, amongst the rest a study of a fir-tree, which looked as if it were cut out of green paper, and a view of his father's house, which he had done entirely by himself, and in which any little defect in perspective was atoned for by a scrupulous attention to detail.

Poor Johnnie handed these one by one to the Squire, his heart beating very fast and his eyes glowing; and the Squire wrinkled up his eyes and twisted his moustache, and said "Ha! ha! ha!" in a way which would have disconcerted any sensitive young artist very much. But Johnnie's skin was of a comfortable thickness, and to his mind the drawings were beautiful; if the Squire did not say much, it was probable that he thought all the more highly of them.

Indeed, he told Johnnie presently that he considered his work quite wonderful, considering his circumstances and opportunities, but at the same time warned him that his plans were impracticable. A great deal of hard study would be required and a good deal of expense incurred before Johnnie could hope to complete his artistic education; and though no doubt a little friendly aid might be forthcoming as regarded the necessary outlay, still his father could not be expected to allow him to adopt a profession in which success was doubtful, and at best must be delayed for long years. Poor

Johnnie, however, pleaded so earnestly and wept so bitterly that at last the Squire promised to see what he could do; and accordingly set out one Sunday afternoon accompanied by the Canon to plead on Johnnie's behalf. Mr. Birch, who was alone, the rest of the family having "stepped across" to a neighbour's, was sitting by a roasting fire in his shirt-sleeves and "stocking feet" enjoying his pipe in the proper Sunday spirit. He listened to everything they urged in absolute silence.

"Well, Birch, what do you say?" asked the Squire, after waiting patiently for a moment or two.

"What do I say, Squire? I say *no*—that's what I say. The lad's my lad I reckon, and I'm going to have summat out of him. I've been workin' all my life an' he may work a bit now. I'm not goin' to slave no more for him to be scribblin' an' messin' wi' 's reds an' blues. He mun ha' done wi' that sort o' work, an' so I tell 'ee, Squire. Theer, that's what I say!"

Not another word could be extracted from him, and the visitors were constrained to retire; the Squire endeavouring to console poor Johnnie (who was anxiously awaiting the result outside) by the present of a sovereign, telling him to buy some oil colours, and paint sign-boards in his spare time.

When the boy entered the house he found his father still thoughtfully smoking with his worsted-clad toes extended to the blaze. "Now, lad," he said, "I've summat to say to ye. Go and fetch me every one o' those picters o' yours—fetch 'em here, I tell 'ee, an' dunnot stan' staring as though ye'd seen a boggart."

"Father, ye wunnot——" pleaded poor Johnnie, turning pale.

"Go, an' fetch 'em I tell 'ee," cried his father, thumping the table heavily with his fist, "or I'll fetch 'em myself, an' if I do it'll be the worse for you. An' fetch your pencils an' paints an' all the rest o' that rubbish."

The boy obeyed slowly and tearfully, and Mr. Birch spreading out all these treasures on the table, wheeled round in his chair and took his pipe out of his mouth. "Now see you here, my lad. I dunnot want to be anyways hard on you, but I mun show ye who's gaffer i' this house. Squire's been here, an' Canon's been here, an' what I've told 'em I tell you. Ye mun ha' done wi'

all that foolery—ye're gettin' a man now, and ye mun give over that nonsense. I've worked 'ard all my life, an' your mother have worked hard—we's be old folk in a few years—an' theer's all that rook o' little un's to do for, an' mostly wenches as isn't fit for much. Now who's to do it ? Who's to work for feyther an' mother when they'n got too old to work for theirsels ? Who but th' oldest lad ? So now, Johnnie, make up your mind to't, for I'll stick to't. You an' me'll start ploughin' to-morrow, an' we'll be done wi' these things once an' for all."

With a sudden quick gesture he swept together all Johnnie's cherished works of art, his paint-box—an old one of the Canon's—his little stock of pencils and paper. Then holding the boy off with one powerful hand, he thrust them into the very heart of the glowing coals, where in a few seconds all were alike destroyed.

Johnnie, in an agony of sobs, wrenched himself away and ran out of the house, and Mr. Birch returned to the enjoyment of his pipe and the contemplation of the fire. Presently his wife came in and began to make preparations for tea ; the small fry dropping in, one by one, and surrounding the table.

"What's gone wi' our Johnnie?" asked Mrs. Birch as she seated herself behind the big brown tea-pot, on which the little folk fixed expectant eyes.

"Eh! he's somewheer about," answered her lord, turning his chair round to the table. · "He'll come in before he's clemmed I daresay."

When the meal was over, however, and it grew dusk, the good woman began to be first angry, and then anxious.

"What*iver* can have come to th' lad? I've niver known him to do such a thing as stay out till this hour. If he's gone foot-ballin' in 's Sunday clothes I'll——"

"Nay, he's none th' lad to go foot-ballin'," interrupted Mr. Birch. "Dunnot ye bother yoursel' about him. He's taken the sulk at summat as I've said, an' wunnot come in till bedtime most like. It's best not to take no notice."

Mrs. Birch was uneasy in her mind, nevertheless, and stole out after putting the children to bed; creeping round the shippons and stack-yard, and calling softly all the time—but no Johnny appeared. It was now nine o'clock, and she became so seriously alarmed that she ran indoors, shook her husband out of his nap, and implored him to take a lantern, and sally forth at once in search of the lad, for she felt sure that something had happened to him. But the father laughed at her fears and refused to budge. If their Johnnie chose to be a fool, let him be a fool. If he didn't want to come in to his good supper and warm bed, let him lie outside with an empty stomach then. It 'ud happen cool him a bit an' do him good.

"But he's got his Sunday clothes on!" sobbed Mrs. Birch. This was the barb to the dart—for her Johnnie to sleep out of doors was bad enough, but to sleep out in his best clothes!

Her husband only growled some inarticulate rejoinder, so Mrs. Birch reduced to the last extremity flung her apron over her head and wept.

Johnnie did not come back that night, nor next day, nor for many days after. His mother was quite heartbroken, but his father was apparently more angry than grieved. He and the neighbours searched far and near, John o' Joe's promising the lad a good thrashing when he caught him; but Johnnie was by this time far beyond the reach of the parental arm, and in spite of all efforts could not be found. It was noticeable that about this time John o' Joe's began to wear what his neighbours called "a down look," and to stoop more than before, and to leave off whistling at his work : his temper too was "shorter" than ever, and much sympathy was felt for poor Mrs. Birch, for it was well known that she could not indulge openly in her grief, her husband having forbidden even the name of the fugitive to be mentioned in his presence.

One cold evening in early winter, about five months after his departure, all the family were assembled at tea, when the latch was suddenly lifted, and Johnnie stood hesitatingly on the threshold. Such a ghost of a Johnnie! pale and thin, and shorn of his thick dark locks; and his clothes, his Sunday clothes! no scare-crow of any respectability would be seen in such things. Mrs. Birch flung her arms round his neck in a passion of mingled joy and anguish, and his brothers and sisters tumbled over each other in their eagerness to welcome him. But his father sat still, and after one steady glance at him, continued to munch his bread and bacon, and to gulp down his tea.

"Eh! feyther, hant ye niver a word for the poor lad?" asked Mrs. Birch tearfully, when the first greetings were over, and she had leisure to observe this attitude of her master's. John Birch finished chewing the morsel in his mouth, swallowed it, and slowly extended his forefinger.

"What's gone wi' 's hair?" he inquired, addressing his wife, and pointing to Johnnie.

"I've just come out o' hospital, feyther; I've had a fever, an' they'n cutt'n it all off," answered the boy for himself.

"Ah!" said John senior, still addressing his wife. "I'm glad to hear as 'twas but in hospital. If 't 'ad ha' been in prison as they'd done it he might spare himsel' th' trouble o' sitting down."

"Come, master, th' lad's whoam at last, an' ye'll

not go for to be 'ard on him. He's had trouble enough I'll reckon."

"Aye, that have I," put in Johnnie timidly. "Eh! feyther, if ye did but know th' 'ardships I've been through ye'd forgive me—ye would, feyther—" beginning to sob—"cold, an' hunger, an' wet—an' 'ard words everywhere."

"Ah!" interrupted John, "it's easy seen why he's comed back—but why did he go?—what took him out of this? That's what I want to know."

"Feyther, I were very wicked an' foolish, but I was mad wi' you for burnin' all my paints an' everythin' I'd done, an' Squire had giv' me a pound an' so I—went off to London, thinkin' I'd get work there and become a great painter."

"An' ye found ye were nobbut a gradely fool," said his father, glancing at him for the first time, "an' ye think as I'm goin' to be another, an' welcome ye back as if ye was th' best son a man could have, i'stead of a thankless lad wi' neither heart nor thought for th' feyther an' mother as done everything for him. I'll do no such thing. Ye went when ye liked, an' ye come back when ye liked—I'm not goin' to say I'm glad to see ye. As ye're here ye can bide—but ye mun work for yer mate—I tell ye that. I'm not goin' to keep ye in idleness. Now, missus, sit ye down, an' give us some more tay."

66

One of the younger children set a chair for Johnnie and his mother put food before him, but the boy's heart was too full to permit him to eat, and after endeavouring for a moment or two to choke down his sobs, he buried his face in his hands and wept bitterly.

John o' Joe's pushed back his chair with a grating noise on the flagged floor, and went out; and the rest of the family endeavoured to console Johnnie. Being still weak and ill, exhausted by his long journey and his recent emotion, it was long before he could control himself sufficiently to relate his story. A pitiful story enough of disappointed hopes and rudely dispelled illusions—poor Johnnie had speedily found his level in the great wilderness of London; and his aspirations were extinguished for evermore. There had been a futile struggle with pride and poverty; hunger, hardship, sickness—and finally the longing for home. He had tramped from London by slow stages, and now— oh!·if his father would only forgive him! How could he ever hold up his head again if he treated him as he had done that night?

"Thy feyther speaks 'arder nor what he feels, I'll tell 'ee that," said Mrs. Birch; "thou mun just tak' no notice an' he'll come round. But thou'll ha' to work, lad—an' no more scribblin'."

No, Johnnie had done with scribbling for good; but as he staggered up to bed it would appear that the

amount of labour to be expected from him for some
time was likely to be small enough.

Nevertheless, morning saw him clad in his working
clothes—which he had much outgrown, by-the-by—and
busy in the farmyard.

His father gave an odd grunt when he found him at
work, but otherwise did not notice him; and presently
the pair sallied forth
together, to plough
up a certain
field ready for
the spring
sowing.

Mr. Birch might
have seen, had he
been a little more on the alert, how feeble were the
lad's steps as they plodded up and down, how pale
was his face, how, in spite of the raw cold, drops of
weakness stood on his brow; but he took no heed of
him beyond an occasional harsh reminder not to go
asleep there, or to lift his legs a bit faster. At last
towards noonday, just as they were turning at the end
of a furrow, Johnnie suddenly let go the horse's head,

staggered sideways with a smothered groan, and fell heavily to the ground.

Then a hoarse cry was heard, and John Birch sprang forward and took the boy in his arms.

"Eh! my lad, my lad!"

A few minutes later Mrs. Birch was startled to see her husband come staggering into the kitchen, carrying Johnnie, whose long attenuated limbs hung apparently lifeless over his arms, while his head drooped upon his shoulder.

"Eh! master, ye've killed him," cried the mother in her anguish.

"I reckon I have, lass," answered John o' Joe's, and then he burst into tears.

But Johnnie was not dead, not he! He soon opened his eyes, and finding himself in his father's arms, flung out his own, and so the two hugged and kissed each other as they had not done since Johnnie was a little fellow in pinafores. Everything was made up after this, and Johnnie soon got strong, and is now a strapping youth, his father's right hand and—not by any means a genius.

NANCY

"Now then, hurry up—that's a good lad! They'll be fair clemmed i' th' field if we dunnot make haste."

"It's mortal 'cavy!" grunted Billy, the curly-pated, crimson-cheeked farm-boy, as he hoisted the great beer-can on his shoulder, and staggered down the garden path in front of his mistress.

"It'll be light enough when yon folks has done wi't," returned Nancy, tilting her sun-bonnet a little more forward, and slinging a large basket covered with a red cotton handkerchief on one sturdy arm.

73

In a few minutes they had left the farm precincts behind, and were marching in single file along a sandy lane bordered on either side by a ragged strip of grass, which gave way in its turn to a deep and muddy ditch.

The brown waters of this were half-covered with some white-starred floating weed, and thickly sown with forget-me-nots and giant marsh marigolds. The air was heavy with the scent of new-mown clover, mingled, occasionally, as they passed some cottage or outlying farmbuilding, with homelier but no less pleasant odours : whiffs from the "shippons," where the sweet-breathed kine were housed for the night; steam from the huge caldron of soaked meal which Granny Gibson was preparing for her pigs; a fine aroma of stable, as Ned Muckworth slouched past with his sleek elephantine team; and from the open door of the last cabin in the straggling village, a smell of frizzling bacon, deemed by Billy so delicious that his youthful heart leaped within him.

"Eh!" he said, with a long-drawn sniff, and tilting the big can dangerously backwards, "they'll be havin' bacon an' taties for supper at Rippons's. I wish I were settin' down wi' 'em, I know."

"If ye dunnot mind ye'll have no supper at all," cried Nancy sharply, as she stretched out her hand to steady the can. "Get along with ye, lazy-bones!"

"I were but havin' a sniff," remonstrated Billy, shambling on again, rather quicker than before; for experience had taught him that when his mistress spoke in that particular tone it was better to keep out of reach of her arm.

"I'll gi' ye summat to sniff at if that's all!" responded Nancy, brandishing her fists with a threatening gesture.

She was a strapping lass, this mistress of Brook Farm, with not much beauty certainly, except that which belongs to vigorous youth and perfect health. Tall, big-framed, and buxom, with a fresh white skin where sun and wind had not browned or hard work reddened it, a pair of plump cheeks that might have vied with the finest apples in her orchard for rosiness, bright blue eyes, and abundant fair hair neatly smoothed under her gathered bonnet. Her gait was free and rapid, her gestures decided, her voice clear and ringing, her tongue of the sharpest. A quick-tempered, keen-witted, rather terrible maiden was Nancy, this notable "wench" who rented the finest farm in the place and whom half the youth of the village had "coorted" in vain. Her father and mother, both of ancient and respectable rustic stock, had married late in life, and had died when Nancy, the sole fruit of their union, was about twenty-two. Nancy had duly wept for them, had worn her "blacks" for the proper time, and had now for three years ruled the farmhouse and the farm itself to the full as cleverly and profitably as her parents had done. Old Gilbertson, her father, had, it was said, saved a tidy bit, Miss Nancy was believed to be possessed of money untold, and the village gossips thought it unhandsome of her to be so obdurate as regarded wedlock, and "to work and slave hersel' to death when she might set down and play the pianney same as any lady i' th' land." But Nancy's tastes did not lie in that direction : she had been brought up with old-fashioned notions of thrift and duty. She perfectly revelled in hard work, and had a fine scorn for folks who hired "slips o' girls to do their business for 'em, as if they hadn't nowt better to do theirsel's nor stitchin' canvas, an' wearin' hats of a week day—walkin' about i' their *shapes*, the idle huzzies!"

This last referred to the new-fangled style of dress,

complete with skirt and bodice, now as frequently seen in the village as the "bed-gown" which Nancy always wore on week-days, as her mother had done before her. It was a far prettier garment than the ill-made gowns at present fashionable among the younger generation. Full, and fresh, and crisp with starch, its lilac folds gathered in at the waist by the string of the wide linen apron, it at once set off the buxom form beneath, and left every movement unimpeded; the short striped petticoat which met it, displayed Nancy's ankles clad in stout stockings of her own knitting; and the well-blacked hob-nailed shoes were designed evidently with a view to comfort rather than elegance. Nancy had as good a stock of laces and ribbons as any one in the country, and a rustling silk dress or two hanging in her cupboard; but she knew better than to put them on on any day but Sunday.

Presently a figure appeared walking at a brisk pace down the lane towards them. A stalwart figure clad in corduroys and velveteen; the bright light of the evening sun shining on hair and flowing beard till they gleamed like gold. This was Martin Rainford, one of the under-keepers, "the gradeliest mon i' th' place," as the village folk said. A fine specimen of a country-man it must be owned, not far off seven feet in his shoes, and broad in proportion. As he drew nearer, his blond face wreathed itself in rather sheepish smiles, and presently he stood stock-still, his gun on his shoulder.

"Evenin's warm," said Nancy, hailing him in her matter-of-fact fashion. "Wunnot ye have a drop o' beer?"

Was such an offer likely to be refused? Martin made one stride towards Billy and the can, tossed off a tumblerful of the amber-coloured liquid in the latter, restored the glass to the boy, wiped his mouth on his sleeve, and nodded to Nancy.

"Goin' whoam?" inquired the latter.

Martin nodded again.

"You're a great stranger, now," observed the girl, with a toss of her head.

"They pheasants," returned Martin, speaking for the first time, and apparently struggling with an over-whelming shyness; "they takes a dale o' looking arter, they do. It's a fine evenin'. Goin' t' th' 'ay-field?"

"Ah. We're workin' till dark. I'm takin' the lads their drinkin'. Good evenin'."

"Evenin'," echoed the taciturn Martin, striding past with the one-sided nod which appeared to be character-istic of him. Nancy almost unconsciously wheeled, and looked after him.

"Eh, yon's a gradely chap!" she said to herself with a half-sigh. "Yon 'ud look well settin' aside of a body i' th' spring cart. An' a-top of an 'ay-rick—my word! he'd be a fine sight!"

A few minutes' brisk walking brought Nancy and Billy to their destination: a big field which was considered the best piece of meadow-land in Brook Farm.

The whole of Nancy's following exerted itself on her behalf this evening, for a treacherous band of clouds marred the gorgeous yellow of the horizon, and there was a flutter and rustle among the leaves that betokened coming rain. Two great carts were being loaded at the further end of the field, and the golden pile on another, opposite the wide-open gate, was being bound with ropes preparatory to removal. The three men in charge of this last-mentioned cart were accommodated first with their portion of the contents of the basket and can, which they disposed of in prodigious gulps, and with all possible despatch.

Nancy, meanwhile, critically surveyed the result of their labours.

"D'ye call that firm an' proper?" she cried, all at once, snatching a pitchfork from the man nearest to her, and raking down the sides of the hay mountain. Three or four tussocks of the sweet-smelling provender fell about her, to the dismay of the hirelings.

"That's *your* notion o' loadin' a cart, is it?" she pursued severely, "leavin' more nor 'alf the stuff i' th' road, enough to keep all the stray cows i' the parish.

For shame of ye, Tommy Treddles—you, as calls your-sel' a man, an' axes for man's wage!"

"Eh, we hadna finished wi't, Missus," expostulated Tommy, a raw and lanky youth, whose red face now peered down from the top of the load.

"What for was ye throwin' rope over it, then, if ye hadna finished?" cried Nancy, gathering up the fallen hay with the pitchfork, and tossing it upwards with vigorous thrusts, to the astonished Tommy. "Theer! happen ye canna heave so high as a wench, you, owd Jack theer, as stands gapin' as though ye'd ne'er seen a pikel afore? Now, Jimmy Norris, catch howd o' th' end o' th' rope, an' let that beer-can be. Theer's others as wants a wet as bad as you, I reckon. Gee back, Di'mond! Hurry up, now, lads; theer's another load i' th' corner, as mun bide till ye coom back."

Diamond strained for a moment with his sleek gigantic limbs, and then the cart went bumping out of the field, followed by Jimmy and Jack still chewing, while Tommy finished his portion of solid meat-pie as he lay outstretched aloft.

Nancy trudged briskly round, her sharp eyes detecting in an instant anything that was amiss; her sharp tongue admonishing and encouraging. The empty cart was trundling back after having deposited its burden at the farm, when she at length turned to go home, Billy preceding her as before.

She walked at a round pace, for it was getting late; the men, in spite of the sustaining "snack" with which she had accommodated them, would, she knew, be hungry for their supper after their hard day's work, and that supper had yet to be prepared.

They proceeded in silence, Billy relieving the tedium of the way by performing a fantasia with his knuckles on the empty beer-can. Nancy absorbed in her own thoughts; so much absorbed, indeed, that it was not till she was quite close to them that she observed a couple walking slowly down the lane in front of her. A man and a woman, the man with his arm passed through the woman's. A big man; a little woman. A woman with a hat, and a much be-frilled and be-ribboned cape; a man with a yellow beard, and a gun on his shoulder. So much she could see in the dusk, and it was quite enough. She passed by them without a word.

"Yon was Mester Rainford and Miss Pratt, wasn't they?" observed Billy presently, looking over his shoulder with a grin. "Her as is ladies'-maid at th' Hall. They're keepin' company this good bit."

"Happen they are," returned his mistress, indifferently. "Now, Billy, my lad, give over hammerin' at that can, or I'll hammer yer head for ye, to a tune as ye wunnot like so well."

Nancy's blighted affections, if blighted they were,

81   F

made no difference either to her appearance or habits: her cheeks were as rosy, her eyes as sharp, her hand as ready as ever, and she looked after her interest with greater zest, if possible, than heretofore.

Hay-making was long over, and reaping, and potato getting; the winter stock of coal was sinking low, and Nancy was beginning to make ready for the young lambs, when there came a spell of stormy weather such as had not been known in these parts for nearly a score of years: strong winds that wrenched the trees upwards by the roots, and laid the hedges flat; and snow that lay thick on the fields and was piled up in mighty drifts in lanes and out-of-the-way corners. In the very middle of this hard weather the foolish, short-sighted little lambs began to make their appearance, and, as was to be expected, after taking a disgusted survey of a very unsatisfactory world, left it again as speedily as might be. The ewes died too, many of them, and Nancy's thrifty soul was wrung within her.

One bleak February morning, when the snow that had fallen during the night lay in dense whiteness over the firmer and less lovely mass beneath, Nancy sallied forth, sustained by clogs and a thick stick, to seek the assistance of a wise old shepherd much respected in the neighbourhood. His cottage stood by itself at the further end of the village, and to reach it Nancy took a short cut across the Squire's park. She stumped along, well muffled in her warm shawl; every step leaving a deep print in the snow; hungry little rabbits, or handsome melancholy pheasants occasionally crossing her path.

Presently she started, for all at once a sort of faint cry fell on her ear. It was scarcely daylight yet, and, with the exception of those already mentioned, there did not appear to be a creature stirring.

She stood still and scanned the white waste of park, with its clumps of trees scattered here and there, and its boundary of gloomy firwood; not a human form in sight; yet the cry which now broke the stillness again was distinctly a human cry.

"In God's name, whatever's that ?" ejaculated Nancy.

She strained her eyes once more, and became suddenly conscious of something unusual in the scene before them.

" Eh ! the great ash ! the half of it's gone ! There's niver some one underneath ! "

The great ash, long so prominent a feature in the landscape, was riven in two, one huge branch having fallen in the night, and being partially covered with snow as it lay on the ground.

Nancy dashed towards it, hearing, as she approached, a low moaning which warned her that her surmise was correct. Lo! beneath the branch lay a figure half-buried in snow, its mighty limbs crushed beneath the weight, its long fair beard entangled in the twigs.

"Martin!" cried the girl, dropping on her knees beside him and trying with all her strength to lift the heavy

bough. But she could not move it one inch, and her sturdy efforts added to his torture.

"Dunnot touch me!" he gasped, "dunnot! I'm all

broke to pieces—an' the snow's been fallin' on me th' whole neet. I mun dee, I doubt."

"Nay, ye shanna!" cried Nancy, bravely. "Not while I'm alive to help you. Bide a bit an' dunnot lose 'eart. I'll fetch a couple o' chaps in a minute as'll be able to carry ye."

She flew off to the village, and presently returned with half a dozen stalwart labourers whom she had captured on their way to the field. They soon removed the branch, and endeavoured, with more good-will than adroitness, to set Martin on his legs—an attention which the hapless giant acknowledged by promptly fainting away.

"Eh, ye great fools!" shouted Nancy. "His leg is broke most like—ye munnot drag at him that gate. Get a shutter, one o' you, or an owd door, an' lay him on't, and shift him so."

After a little delay a door was procured; Nancy, meanwhile, covering the injured man with her shawl, and supporting his head on her knee.

"Wheer mun we take him to?" asked one of the bearers as they prepared to start. "We'll niver be able to carry him so far as the Lone End wheer he lodges. He's mortal 'eavy, an' looks as though he wur goin' to dee."

"'Take him to my place, then," said Nancy. "It's nearest, I reckon, an' I'll see as he's well done to."

The doctor shook his head over Martin: he was nearly, as he said himself, "broken to pieces." One arm and one leg were fractured so badly that amputation was necessary: several ribs were broken: there seemed to be no end to the damage which the poor fellow had sustained. Nancy and old Kitty, her factotum, nursed him with devotion, if not precisely tenderness, for many weeks. Miss Pratt visited him once, but her susceptibilities were apparently so much shocked by the sight of this wreck of a man that she did not repeat the attention.

Rainford's parents were both dead, and he had no near "kin" to fall back on, therefore Nancy's good offices were the more valuable.

As time passed and it was known "for certain" that Martin would never be fit for work again, much curiosity was aroused in the village as to what Nancy's plans might be with regard to him. Did she mean to keep him always at the farm—"a poor do-less creature as could scarce so much as dress himsel'?" And was it not rather a queer thing, said some of the more severe, for a wench same as her to make such a to-do with a chap like yon? Heads began to shake and tongues to wag over Nancy's proceedings, and one fine day her maternal aunt drove up in her shandry to remonstrate with her.

Poor Martin, white-faced and melancholy, with his clothes clinging loosely round his shrunken form, his empty right sleeve pinned to his breast, while a rug hid his solitary lower limb, was installed on a couch by the kitchen fire; therefore, after exchanging a few commonplace remarks with him, Mrs. Wilcox conveyed to her niece, by various telegraphic nods and winks, her desire to speak to her privately.

They adjourned to the parlour, and the elder woman proceeded to the point at once.

"He do look bad, for sure!" she remarked. "How's he goin' to get's livin' when he leaves this?"

"I dunno," responded Nancy, composedly.

"If he was to go to Liverpool he might pick up a few pence, sweeping a crossin', happen," suggested her relative cheerfully. "Or maybe they'd take him in a show—wi' th' whole o' one side gone I may say, an' him so big an' tall, they might do summat wi' him. I've seen sights as was less curious. Eh, poor chap! They say as when folks has their limbs chopped off they dunnot lose feelin' in 'em for iver such a time. Did ye see Martin's arm when th' doctor cut it off—or's leg?"

"Nay," returned Nancy, quickly. "I'd summat better to do, I reckon, nor be gapin' at such like."

"I'd 'ave liked to see 'em," pursued her relative, tranquilly. "Lord o' me! I mind when owd Jem

Seddon had's fingers whipped off wi' th' steam saw, he picked 'em up wi's other hand an' wrapped 'em i' paper so nice and tidy, an' took 'em whoam. I met him i' th' road an' I said: 'Eh, whatever's th' matter, Jem; you look all of a shake?' An' for all he were feelin' so bad he had to laugh. 'What do ye think as I've got 'ere?' he says. 'I can't tell, I'm sure,' I says. 'A handful o' fingers,' says he, an' he opens out the parcel an' shows me, quite proud, th' poor chap! Eh! the whole village had to see Jem's fingers—An' ye niver so much as axed to look at Martin's arm!—Well, there'll be a to-do wi' him when he leaves this, I reckon, but it cannot be helped. Ye'll have to get him out o' your road here, soon, anyway."

"I can do with him!" said Nancy, folding her arms a trifle defiantly.

"Aye, but there's a dale o' talk about him an' you already," returned Mrs. Wilcox with a sudden change of tone. "People wonders at ye for keeping of him here—him as is no kin to you, no, nor your equals nayther. If you'd ha' been keepin' company it 'ud ha' been different, but him as was coortin' Miss Pratt yonder at th' Hall! Eh, if you'd ha' heerd all as folks are sayin'—an' it's none such nice hearin' for your mother's sister nayther, I can tell you." Here Mrs. Wilcox evinced a disposition to weep.

"I dunnot care a brass farden for what folks say!"

cried her niece, snapping her finger and thumb. "Not that! I'm not goin' to turn th' poor lad out on th' road for anybody. Tell Polly Birch she needn't think she'll see the straighter for making out as other people has crooked eyes. I know what that long tongue o' hers is; at the bottom of any mischcevious work as is agate. But I can let mine wag a bit too, happen, and then we'll see!"

"Poor Polly Birch only spoke i' kindness!" expostulated the matron.

"I can do wi' less kindness, then. Are you goin' to th' village now? Will you have a cup o' tea first?"

But Mrs. Wilcox was too much hurt and offended to accept of any hospitality, and she drove off, baffled and heated, leaving Nancy totally unconvinced.

It was a different matter, however, when the Canon spoke to her on the subject. Nancy had a great respect for the Canon, and when she spied him walking up the little flag-paved garden path her face beamed. He was smiling, too, at his own thoughts. But now he composed his features.

"I want a quiet word with you, Nancy."

"Do ye, Canon?"

"Yes. About Martin Rainford, you know. What are you going to do with him?"

"There's not much as can be done wi' him, as I know," responded Nancy, her manner stiffening a little, and the smiles vanishing. "Doctor says as when he gets a bit stronger he mun have a wooden leg ; his ribs is mendin'—but his arm's took right off up by the shoulder—there's nowt as can be done for that. He'll niver be fit for work again, I doubt."

"Well, but Nancy, he can't stay here, you know. He's no relation of yours and you are too young to look after him as you do. People will talk—they are talking already."

"I care nowt i' they are. 'Ard words break no boans, Canon. What's the poor chap to do? He mun have some one to do for him—he can scarce so much as feed himsel'—an' he's no kin i' th' place."

"Well, he must go to the workhouse, I'm afraid. You can't keep him, Nancy. Come, be sensible! No young woman can take charge of a young man like that, unless—unless she is married to him."

"Eh, Canon!" cried Nancy, indignantly. "Married! Why yon's but half a mon, poor fellow! Who'd wed wi' him?"

The Canon looked sharply at her.

"Who indeed? Was there not something between him and one of the maids at the Hall?"

"Miss Pratt"—contemptuously. "I doubt she'll think no more o' poor Martin now. She came here nobbut once to see him, howdin' up her skirts an' cockin' her nose i' th' air when she passed the midden—an' it made up wi' fine wholesome farmyard muck as it 'ud please any one to sniff at. And when she saw Martin, she hollered out as she were goin' to faint. 'Nay,' I says, 'I canna do wi' faintin's here!' An' our Kitty smacked her 'ands till she come to pretty quick. But she niver come since."

"We might get up a little subscription for him," said the Canon meditatively. "I'm sure the Squire would help—perhaps he need not go to the workhouse after all—he might lodge somewhere——"

"It mun be somewheer as he'll be well done to, then," put in Nancy. "He wants lookin' arter same as a babby a'most. Who's goin' to be at th' trouble o' that?"

"Well, well, we must see what can be done—but bear in mind what I tell you, Nancy. He must get out of this. I'm not going to have any more scandal-mongering about him."

The Canon nodded and went away, leaving Nancy in an unusually reflective mood.

Miss Pratt had just finished dinner, and was sitting in the housekeeper's room, toying with a strip of crochet-work and flirting with the footman—just to keep her hand in—when a message was brought to her that Miss Gilbertson wanted to see her.

"Won't you step in?" said Miss Pratt, tripping to

the back door, where Nancy stood, her large back in its print bedgown turned towards the house.

"No, thank ye," said Nancy, whisking round: she had been shaking her fist at the yard dog, which was straining at its chain and barking itself hoarse, presumably tantalised at the sight of her sturdy unprotected ankles. "I want nobbut a word wi' ye."

"Oh!" said Pratt, contemptuously surveying the stalwart figure, in its unfashionable gear, and giving a little shake to her own smart silk dress which was intended to provoke envy. Nancy snorted: she was not going to dress up for the likes of her, and knew that a single one of her fine pigs was worth more than the whole of Miss Pratt's wardrobe; but the action irritated her nevertheless. She looked defiantly at the sneering abigail.

"It's just this. What are ye goin' to do about Martin Rainford?"

"About him," cried the other, starting and flushing; "what about him?"

"Ah—that's wheer it is. What about him? Ye have not troubled yoursel' so much about him, have ye? He's doin' pretty fair, doctor says, an' 'll soon be fit for's wooden leg. But he'll niver work no more. What's to be done wi' him? He's no kin to nobody 'ere, an' he mun have some one to do for him. You an' him had best wed as soon as you can, an' then ye

can see to him proper. Ye'll not have saved much o'
your wage, I doubt "—with a scornful glance that took
in Miss Pratt, from her frizzled head to her high-heeled
shoes—" Ye'll not have a dale to start housekeepin' on ;
but ye can take in washin', an' fat pigs, an' that "—
Miss Pratt's face was a study—" Ye'll not be the first
woman as has had her husband to keep."

There was a dead silence. Presently the maid asked,
with a toss of her head, if Martin had sent Nancy with
this message.

"Nay. I'm not goin' to run of errands for anybody.
I coom o' mysel'. Well, what d'ye say ? The lad's got
to be looked to, an' Canon says as he munna stay
longer wi' me. He's been well done to theer, though I
say it ; an', if he mun go, he mun ha' somebody to take
care of him. Well, Miss Pratt ? "

"Well, Miss Gilbertson, I'm very sorry, I'm sure,
that you can't keep Martin any longer, and I'm very
sorry for him, too, poor fellow. Very, very sorry—but
what can I do ? I—I could not think of taking such
a responsibility on myself. I'm not equal to it ; and
besides, I don't think Martin could expect any one to
marry him now. Really, the very ideer is shockin' !
Besides, for some time I'd been doubting if I was suited
to him, if I could make him 'appy. Indeed I've other
views at present. I don't mind telling you, Miss
Gilbertson, that I'm engaged to a very superior young

man, an English gentleman of Irish extraction, called Murphy. Him an' me——"

"An' what's to become o' Martin?" put in Nancy, who apparently took no interest in Miss Pratt's plans except in so far as they regarded the ex-keeper.

"Really, I can't be expected to know. He must lodge somewhere, I suppose."

"Canon says as he'll most like have to go to the workhouse," observed Nancy, stolidly.

"Well, perhaps, that would be the best thing for the poor fellow in the long run—as he can't work," returned Miss Pratt, in a tone of relief. "They take very good care of people there, I believe, and we could go and see him and bring him tobacco, you know. Poor Martin loves his pipe"—with a sigh of sentimental reminiscence.

Nancy raised her blue eyes, which positively burned with scornful anger, and, moreover, lifted her sturdy arm with so fierce a gesture that the little maid skipped hastily backwards.

"For shame of ye," cried Nancy, snapping her fingers close to the other's nose. "For shame of ye, ye dirty little slut!"

Thereupon Miss Pratt shut the door in her face, and went into hysterics behind it, and the mistress of Brook Farm trudged homewards.

She found that the dough for her weekly bread-making had run over the great brown pans, and her anxiety to repair this mishap at first swallowed up all other thoughts. Presently, however, as she kneaded the solid mass, punching it and rolling it in her usual vigorous style, her eyes fell on Martin, installed as usual on the couch, spelling over a week-old newspaper. The couch had been rolled to the open window, partly to leave more room for Nancy's bread-making operations, and partly that the sweet April air might refresh the invalid. An apple-tree in blossom was waving its branches without in the breeze, a row of hyacinths in glasses decorated the window-sill, the birds were singing cheerily, and men were calling to each other in the adjacent field. A great farm-horse passed the window, with clanking harness and slow, ponderous tread, followed by Billy, cracking his whip and whistling. There was a pleasant stir and bustle—the bustle of spring—everywhere. Nancy sighed.

"If it mun be done, it mun be done," she said to herself; and then aloud:

"Did I tell ye as Canon's been here to-day?"

"Nay," said Martin, turning his head. "I wonder he didn't look in to ax how I were. He has not been here this while back."

"He were talkin' of ye though," said Nancy. "Plenty. He thinks you ought to clear out o' this soon, and wants to know what ye're goin' to do with yoursel'."

"What I'm goin' to do?" repeated Martin, his face clouding over. "He may well ax. There's nowt as I can do, only ate other folks' stuff, and lay heer same as a log o' wood."

"Ye'll be able to get about more when you've got your wooden leg. But ye mun have a woman to see to ye, an' Canon says it had ought to be your wife!"

"Wife! Whativer's that ye say? Who'd take up wi' a broken-down chap like me?"

"I went to Miss Pratt at th' Hall," said Nancy, "and axed her straight if she were goin' to be's good as her word an' get married to ye, an' work for ye, same as you'd ha' done for her, if ye hadn't have had this accident. An' she said as she couldn't think o' such a thing an' was keepin' company wi' some other chap now."

Here Nancy withdrew her arms from the dough, folded them, and looked with her sharp, direct gaze at Martin. She had said her say—part of it at least—without wasting time in preliminaries; and Martin, though he looked gloomy enough, seemed by no means surprised.

"Aye," he said after a pause. "I misdoubted me that she were up to summat o' th' sort. Her an' me had words the very neet as tree fell o' me. I misdoubted me then—it were that, I think, as made me walk reet under that rotten owd ash tree wi' th' wind blowin'

enough to deave one, an' th' snow that thick as if
I'd ha' had my senses I'd have cut away whoam
i'stead o' loiterin' i' th' park. But I couldn't give
over thinkin' o' that wench an' her ways; I was fair
moidered."

"Ah, she's not one to moider hersel' wi' thinkin' o'
you, then. 'Happen he'd best go to th' workhouse,' she
says."

"Did she say that?" asked Martin quickly.

"Aye, she did."

"Well, happen it is the best thing I could do."

There was a moment's silence, and then he struck the
window-sill savagely with his solitary fist.

"I wish yon tree 'ad done a bit more damage while
'twas about it," he said. "I wish it 'ad cracked my
crown. The kindest service as any one could do me
now 'ud be to stick a cartridge i' that owd gun o' mine,
as I's never carry no more, an' put muzzle t' my ear an'
blow my brains out. I'm nowt but cumber, nowt else;
an' I'm nobbut twenty-six! Eh, Lord! It's an awful
thing for the half of a body to dee afore th' t'other half.
It fair drives me mad to think on't. Happen I'll live
fifty year more. Everybody wishing me dead an' mysel'
most of all."

Nancy carefully wiped her floury hands in her apron,
stalked across the kitchen, and possessed herself of
Martin's sturdy palm.

"Speak for yoursel'," she said, with a queer sort of laugh ; "I dunnot wish ye dead, Martin, an' I hope wi' all my heart as ye *will* live fifty year. It needn't be in th' workhouse when all's said an' done."

"Aye, but wheer mun I go? Canon says I mun be flitting from here——"

"Nay, he did not altogether say that. He says : 'Nancy, ye can't do for yon chap same as you're doin' now, for iver. Ye're too young. He should have a wife to look arter him.' Well, an' then I went an' axed Miss Pratt same as I told ye——"

"Aye, an' ye found as she cared nowt for me, an' for that matter I care nowt about her, now."

"Well, I'll tell ye plain, Martin, as I always thought to do pretty well for mysel' when I did wed, I always said as I'd have nobbut a gradely chap for my master : one as could work a bit for himsel', an' gaffer the men, an' that. Now you, as ye say, 'll niver be fit for much i' this world—unless happen," said Nancy, with a provident eye to the future, "ye could cut up a two-three seed potatoes, an' feed the hens, an' such-like."

"Aye," said Martin calmly, "I could do that, belike—an' I could gaffer the lads too. I can shout a bit still—an' my eyesight's as strong as iver't were."

"Ah, but they'll niver think so much of a master as

has but one leg," pursued Nancy, gazing at him with an appraising eye. "Eh, an' nobbut one arm, an' that the left! It'll look rale bad when ye're sittin' at th' head o' th' table at harvest supper that ye should have but the left arm to drink 'calths wi'!"

"Ah!" sighed poor Rainford, his face, which had brightened up for a moment during the discussion, darkening again. "It will that. I doubt it's no use, Nancy, my lass. I'll niver make a fit mate for ye. But I thank ye truly all the same, an' take it very kind o' ye to ax me."

"Wait a bit, I've more to say yet. Martin Rainford, the fust time I see ye, I says to mysel', 'Yon's th' man for my money.'"

"Did ye?" said Martin, with a sheepish smile.

"Aye, ye was a fine-set-up fellow i' those days. Well, I'd ha' liked ye then well enough; an' though I may say as the best part o' ye is gone, I'm none o' th' kind that's always choppin' an' changing'—so if ye're willin' I'll make a shift to do wi' ye as ye are."

POLITICS

"COME in, ma'am," says Mrs. Wick, "come in and sit ye down. It's a long time since you've come our way. Ah, the elections kept ye busy? Indeed they're enough to moider anybody—we hear too much of 'em here, I can tell you. Specially since we've changed our politics. Didn't ye know as we'd changed our politics here in the village, ma'am? Eh dear, yes; and it has been a piece of business ever since, what with one side an' t'other when the elections comes round.

"Squire began it, you know. Him an' his family has always been Liberals—always used to be at least— and of course *we* was Liberals too. Well, last election time—not the last as ever was, but the time before—or was it the time before that again? he went an' turned round and said he was goin' to vote for the Conservative party. Eh, well, to think of it! we all said, and whatever could have come to the Squire! It seemed funny, ye know. Us women couldn't talk of nothing else, and the men said the notion seemed to stick in their throats

—maybe that was why they was always walkin' off to the public-house to wash it down! One man—Radical Ted as we call him—made a great to-do about it, and said *he* wasn't goin' to turn his coat inside out, not for nobody. But none of us ever minded poor old Ted.

"Squire called a meetin' in the big barn up yonder, and made a speech. It was a beautiful speech, ah! indeed it was, and he talked to us so nice about why he'd changed his views, or rather, says he, it's the times that has changed. The old Liberalism is a thing of the past, and the Conservative policy of the present day is the nearest thing to the Liberal policy that you and me was brought up on, says the Squire. And he said he was very much disappointed in the Grand Old Man. 'In fact,' says he, leanin' on his stick, an' looking round, 'my opinion is that he is a grand old Humbug.' And then he talked to us as friendly as possible, about this kind of Government and that kind of Government— there wasn't many of us as understood it all—and he finished up by sayin' that the Liberals were Illiberal, and the Conservatives Preservative. Eh, you should have heard us cheerin' him! My word! you'd have thought the roof was comin' off. Some of us fancied he was goin' into Parliament himself, but he says he was too old for that. He was informed, however, that the gentleman who was going to stand for our division of the county was a very nice young gentleman indeed. We'd have an opportunity of judging for ourselves soon, he says, because he was coming to hold a meetin' here, and he was sure we'd all attend, and now he'd shown us why he had changed his opinions he hoped we'd all follow suit. Well, we all cheered again, and poor old Joseph Birch, the carpenter, sings out, 'For he's a jolly good fellow,' as he always does whenever he gets a chance, for he sets a deal of store by the Squire.

"A few days after a gentleman comes round the village, a very nice gentleman he was—first we thought it must be him as Squire was talkin' of, but he says no, he was only a mutual friend—an' he sits down an' talks to us as natural as possible, an' praises Squire till the tears comes into his eyes, an' he says we mustn't on no account vote for the Liberals because if we do the agricultural interests of the country will be ruined, and Irishmen will be takin' the bread out o' the mouths of Englishmen.

"We all said that 'ud be terrible, and we'd try and attend the meetings, an' that, but it was a busy season, and we didn't know if we could so very well spare the time. 'What!' says the gentleman, quite astonished, 'would you run the risk of ruining your country for the sake of an hour's work more or less? Get up a bit earlier in the morning,' he says, turnin' pleasant again.

107

Well, then he gets out a card with two names on it. One printed very big—and that was his and Squire's gentleman—and the other very small.

"'Now,' he says, 'you can't make any mistake. See *this* is the name you are to put your mark opposite to.'

"'Oh,' says we, turnin' it about. 'The big · one—we'll remember.'

"'No, no, no,' says the gentleman, very flurried. 'Never mind whether it's big or little—it's the name you've got to remember.' And he shouts it out a dozen times, and spells it, and makes us spell it, till we're sick of the sound of it. 'Now you can't forget,' he says.

"The very next day another of 'em comes, and sits down and talks. Tells us what fine people we are, and how honest and independent we've always been, and how if we'll only vote right we'll enjoy greater prosperity than ever. Then *he* pulls out a card with one name printed very big and one name printed very little.

"'Oh, thank ye,' says we, 'the other gentleman left us one o' those.'

"'What other gentleman?' says he, and he stops for a minute, and then he says, 'would you kindly let me have a look at it?'

"Well, when it's fetched, he looks real put out.

'Why this is the wrong one,' he says, 'You'll be gettin' muddled up if you keep this. See, *this* is the name of the people's friend—the friend of the farmer and the labourer,' he says. 'The friend o' cheap bread and high wages, and short hours,' he says, an' he shows us *his* card, an' the big name was a strange name, an' the t'other—the name o' the Squire's gentleman—was wrote quite small and poor.

" ' *This* is the name you've got to remember,' says he, p'intin' to the strange one.

" ' Nay,' says we. 'It was the t'other, Squire told us.'

" ' And are you going to be so poor-spirited as to follow your Squire's lead just like a flock of geese?' says he. 'Your Squire indeed ! So he's been tampering with your liberties, has he ? Do you suppose *he* has your interests at heart, or cares two pins for you, except for what he can get out of you ? What can you expect from a man who has a wall round his place to shut out the people, when the land should by right belong to the people, and will do so yet if they have the courage to be true to themselves.'

" ' Eh well,' says one of us, ' we know the Squire, ye see, an' we'd rayther vote for a friend of his, nor for a gentleman as we've never heerd on. An' I doubt it's no worse for Squire to have a wall to's place, nor for me to have a hedge to my garden. An' ye can leave

109

your card if ye like aside of t'other on the chimney-piece.'

" And so he did after a deal more talk and argument,

and there stood the cards side by side till one of the young ladies from the Hall chanced to see them.

" 'It's no use keeping two,' she said. 'You'll only be making mistakes. Better put this one into the fire.'

"So into the fire she pops it, and round she goes to every house in the place, and does the same by every one o' the cards as the last gentleman left. My word! there *was* a piece of work when some of his lady friends heerd on it. Eh! we was always havin' visitors that time! We got to be quite moidered in the end; not so much as Saturday would go by but some one or other would walk in, in the middle of our cleaning up—the children half washed and all—with ' How do ye do?' and 'I hope we may count on you.' ' No,' says we, ' don't count on us, we've other things to be thinkin' on.' We were gettin' vexed at the end, ye see—and then they said they did like our fine independent spirit. One of that lot took to sending soup to old Granny Gibson (as if she hadn't sons and grandsons to work for her and keep her comfortable), and Granny says nothin' —not even Thank ye —so one day they axed her if she got it all right.

" ' Ah,' says Granny, ' I got it reet enough. Gave it to the pigs, I did,' says Granny. So after that they sent no more.

" One day there was a deal of stir in the village— some one had been talkin' about three acres and a cow as they heerd was to be given to any one as voted against Squire's gentleman. Well, ye may think the cottagers had something to say about this—none of their gardens run to more nor half an acre at most, and as for cows, it's only the gradely farmers as keeps them. There was more talk about that nor anything else; even old Joseph the carpenter, as never wants anything new, and shakes his head at all these election

111

doin's, even he said it would be very nice. But Squire
come into his workshop—'So you're to have three acres
and a cow, Joe?' says he, and he laughs fit to split.
'And who is going to build your shippons, I wonder?
I'm sure I shan't,' he says.

"And then Joseph 'unbethought himself,' as he
always says, and says he: 'What's the good o' goin'
agin the Squire? I won't deny that three acres o' land
is nice, an' so's a cow—very nice. But who is this here
chap as is goin' to give them to us, an' what do we
know about him? And the Squire's been a good squire
to us, an' a good friend to us—and theer! What's the
good o' goin' agin him?'

"Well, Joseph was right, ye see, and there wasn't
one here in the village as would say he wasn't, for all
the talk we heard about Liberty, and every man being
as good as his better, and that. Us an' the Squire was
always friends. We all know him, and he knows us,
and his ways is ours.

"After a bit the young gentleman as we'd all heerd
so much on—him as Squire was going to vote for, ye
know—come to hold a meetin' here. But he gave short
notice, and the very day of the meetin' was Dumbleton
Fair day, the biggest fair in the country, as all farmers
attend regular. There was messengers flyin' all over
the place, tellin' every one to come, and as many as
could make time did come to the barn where the gentle-

man was to speak. A good few women was there, and almost all the big school children, but the men was most of them busy, and I doubt if there was more nor half a dozen of them there, all told. But the barn was done up elegant with plants and flowers and decorations of all sorts, and when the young gentleman came out to speak, he look round and smiled to hisself. He began by sayin' how beautiful everything was done up, and how kind it was o' the Squire to have all so nicely prepared, and then he went on in a kind o' sneery way to remark what a pity it was as the attendance didn't correspond with the decorations. The men sat there smilin' as if it all was as pleasant as could be, but I gave Mrs. Birch, as sat next me, a nudge.

"'What d'ye think o' that?' says I.

"'Eh,' says she, 'I don't make much count o' yon flipperty-gibbet. When's Squire goin' to speak?'

"Eh, but the t'other talked our heads off afore he'd done, an' when Squire clapped his hands, we clapped ours, but we *was* glad when he stopped. Then the gentleman as came round with the cards, spoke, and another after that, and then at last Squire come to the front.

"'Hear, hear!' cries Joseph, afore he'd said a word at all; and the rest of us hammered the floor with our umberellas, an' shuffled our feet and clapped our hands; an' Squire nods at us, an' laughs.

"His speech was the best; we all was agreed on that p'int. Afterwards him and his young gentleman come round the village—he had a smile an' a joke for every one, had the young gentleman—very pleasant he was. He says to Radical Teddy: 'You're bound to vote for me, you know. Why, you carry my colours in those blue eyes of yours.'

"'An' what colour do I wear here?' says Ted, tappin' his nose. 'I'm a red republican,' says Ted (he gets them out-landish words out o' the newspapers, ye know).

"Talkin' of colours— the day of the elections them ladies as I told ye of—as sent Granny Gib-son soup, waited for the children as they was comin' out from school, and pinned bows o' ribbon on 'em, boys and girls alike— beautiful they was. But when our own young ladies— the ladies from the Hall saw them, they *were* in a way.

114

" 'The idea,' says they, 'of plastering *our* children with their disgusting Radical ribbons.' And they whipped them off before you could turn round, and popped on blue ones. And the children looked fine as they stood at the end o' the village, cheerin' the voters when they passed. First there was the Squire driving his dog-cart, as pleased as Punch, with a blue bow in his button-hole, and blue ribbons on the horse; and then come the farmers' shandries, and after them come waggons—as the farmers lent for the occasion—with all the cottagers, an' off they drove, cheerin' all the way, an' every man in the place voted for Squire's gentleman. Radical Ted come back so drunk that he couldn't tell us much about it, and he always said he couldn't remember which way he voted, but of course we all knew without the tellin' that he'd never go for to vote again the Squire. An' that's how we all changed our politics here in this village, ma'am; now you have the whole story."

"THE GILLY-F'ERS"

THERE is perhaps nothing of which the inhabitants of Thornleigh are more proud than the stocks which adorn their village green. Some time ago the elders among them could even remember the days when poachers and tramps and drunkards used to be confined in them, and pelted by the youth of the neighbourhood with cabbages and rotten eggs. But it is long since the stocks—as an institution —were used in Thornleigh, and for years no one but old Jack Rutherford — " Gillyf'er Jack," as he was called— ever sat on the queer old bench

which former generations had polished till it gleamed again. He found it a convenient resting-place sometimes while he munched his " baggin'," for it was in the neighbourhood of his work, and moreover a sunny and cheerful spot. When Jack was not digging a grave for anybody, or ringing the church bell, or cutting wall-flowers, he earned his living by mending the roads. That is to say, in summer he swept up the dust, and in winter he scooped the water out of the puddles with his shovel; and sometimes he found an old shoe or two or a brimless hat, which came in handy for filling up the ruts; or if he chanced upon a *very* bad piece, he scratched up a few stones out of a more level portion and laid them in the deepest holes. The Thornleigh people did not like paying rates, and Jack never had anything to mend the roads with; therefore the Local Board thought he did very well as it was, and so did Jack himself, and the Squire (who was chairman) laughed when he found himself nearly bounced out of his dog-cart, and said it was good for the liver to be jolted a bit.

Jack's home was quite at the further end of the village—a one-storied red cottage, so old that the walls formed all kinds of curious curves and angles, and every variety of moss and lichen appeared to flourish on the thatch. The small-paned windows were almost filled up with scarlet geraniums, and the tiny garden without was bright with sweet-williams and stocks and old-fashioned moss and cabbage-roses. The sweet, cool, delicious little monthly rose, too, bloomed gaily there nearly all the year round. But the pride of Jack's heart and the chief source of his income was the little field of wall-flowers, or, as they are called in Thornleigh, "gilly-f'ers," which lay at the back of his house. Wall-flowers of every shade from brightest yellow to deepest chocolate-brown—rows and rows of them. Poor old Jack's back ached as he waded among them when they were in season, his clasp-knife crunching through their leafy stalks, the basket on his arm growing fuller and heavier, till at last it could hold no more, and Jack, straightening himself and sighing, would slouch over to Margery, turning out the sweet-smelling heap on the table where she sat "bunching" them for market. They *were* sweet! The scent of them used to hang over the entire village. Every one knew Jack's gilly-f'er field—it was quite a feature in the place. Neighbours passing to and fro and farmers driving by would point out the "gilly-f'ers" to each other, till at last the cottage itself, and even the old couple to whom it belonged, came to be known by that name. Margery, indeed, considered as an individual and not as her husband's better-half, could not have claimed any special title, but collectively they were called "The Gilly-f'ers," and "Gilly-f'er Jack" was as well known in the neighbourhood of Thornleigh as the stocks themselves.

Margery was the most motherly of wives, and was accustomed to devote much of her time and thoughts to the education of Jack; and "certainly," as she said emphatically many a time, "if he did not know his duty it would not be for want of hearing about it." As a rule Jack obeyed her in all things, even to taking off his clogs before he crossed his own threshold and to wearing one of his wife's aprons on Sundays to preserve his best clothes. But unfortunately in one or two points he fell short of her ideal. There was his pipe, to begin with. In spite of everything Margery could say he would persist in " wearin' his brass " on baccy, and many a sly whiff did he enjoy seated on a corner of the stocks after a furtive glance round to make sure that his " missus " was not in sight. There were occasions too—few and far between, for as a rule Jack was "as sober a man as a woman need be tied to "—when he was known to be a little " overtaken." At Christmas-time perhaps a neighbour would treat him to a glass, which immediately affected his head, or rather his legs ; and on Club-day—oh, Club-day was, as Margery said, a snare ! Jack, of course, ribbon in coat and wand in hand, marched round the country with the other members of the Thornleigh and Little Upton Mutual Benefit Club, the band playing merrily, and the big banner, with the Squire's arms on one side and a picture of the Good Samaritan on the other, streaming in the breeze ; and of course everybody had beer ; and of course—poor Jack !

Margery had " bethought hersel' " and " unbethought

hersel'" often about this Club. It was undoubtedly a
good thing to belong to it. If Jack were sick she
could draw ten shillings a week from the Club funds
till he was able to resume work again, and when he
died the Club would hand over quite a nice little sum
towards his funeral. On the other hand, besides his
subscription, he was obliged to contribute, like all the
other members, towards the annual dinner at the
Thornleigh Arms; and, having paid for his share of
the good cheer, it was only fair that he should partake
of it. Margery's just and economical soul rebelled at
the idea of sacrificing his rights, and yet it was always
the same story. On this particular day every year
Jack forgot himself, and during the remaining three
hundred and sixty-four Margery reminded him of his
slip. At last she made up her mind to take a decisive
step, and, renouncing with a struggle the value of that
annual two-and-sixpence, resolved to keep her husband
at home in future when other folk went "pleasurin'."

Accordingly, when Jack woke up one Club-day
morning, he found no shining suit of broadcloth laid
out by his bed, no wand, no be-ribboned hat—only his
working clothes lying in a heap just as he had taken
them off.

"Hullo!" he cried cheerfully, "what's gone wi' your
membry, missus? To-day's Club-day. Wheer's my
Sunday clothes?"

"I know what day it is well enough," returned Margery from the adjoining kitchen. "But you're going to none o' their clubs to-day, so ye'll not need your good clothes. Get into the t'others now, and come to your breakfast. It's late enough."

"I'm not goin' to the Club?" repeated Jack in amazement. "An' what am I not goin' to the Club for?—me as has walked this thirty year."

"What should ye not go for?" cried Margery shrilly, and then came a bang and clatter of crockery as she prepared for battle. "D'ye mean to tell me you've forgot——"

While she reminded him at length, and in vigorous language, of his misdemeanours of last year and the years preceding it, Jack hunted about for his clothes. But the cupboard was locked and Margery had the key in her pocket. What was to be done? Was he to give up without a murmur the one pleasure of his life—the outing to which, for as long as he could remember, he had looked forward from year's end to year's end? Be considered a backslider by his fellow-members and become the laughing-stock of the country-side? It was not to be borne.

Just as Margery was working up with great animation to "this time five year ago," the inner door was partially opened, and Jack's wrinkled face, flaming with anger, was thrust through the chink.

"I mun ha' my clothes, woman! Hand over yon key an' let's ha' no more to do. I'll ha' them, or else go i' th' t'other ones. I tell ye plain I'm goin', so it bides wi' you whether I'm to go decent or no."

"John Rutherford, you're out o' your senses I doubt!" exclaimed Margery. "Pretty doin's indeed for you to be bargin' at your wife, that gait! Get on wi' them clothes an' give over saucin' me. For shame of ye! Ye don't go to your Club to-day, an' ye needn't look for it. Your Sunday suit shall bide i' th' cupboard, an' as for goin' i' th' t'others, I reckon ye know better nor make a sight o' yoursel' at this time o' day, an' ha' th' children shoutin' after ye i' th' lane——"

Jack banged the door to again, and lost the remainder of his wife's speech. He sat down on the side of the bed, trembling with rage, but, for once in his life, determined. He was not going to be put off with Margery's nonsense, and would go to the Club, clothes or no clothes, if it was only to shame her. After a moment or two he rose and began to assume his ordinary gear with a solemn face and a sore heart. Things was come to a pretty pass indeed when he, John Rutherford, the oldest member of the Club, was forced to attend the meeting in such "togs" as these! He thought of how Margery herself had hitherto always helped him to array himself with becoming splendour;

125

how she had brushed his coat and fastened his cravat and tied on his ribbons with wifely pride and care; and now she served him like this!

He looked so subdued when he at length came into the kitchen that the woman's heart smote her in the midst of her elation at what she took to be her victory.

"Sit thee down," she said gently, pushing forward a chair.

"Nay, I'll not sit me down, Margery Rutherford," said Gilly-f'er Jack, "an' I want none o' yer coffee. I'm goin' to the Club. Folks 'ull soon know the kind o' wife I've got. I'm goin' to shame ye for once— that's what I'm goin' to do—I'm goin' to shame ye."

He thrust his feet into the great clogs which lay in the chimney-corner and shambled out of the house, Margery listening vaguely to the clump-clump of his step till it was lost in the distance. She was too much astonished at first to realise the full meaning of her husband's threat; but after a time it dawned upon her that before nightfall the history of their quarrel would be known all over the place, and that probably most of the neighbours would be weak minded enough to take Jack's part.

When her morning's work was over, and she had "cleaned her" and donned a fresh apron, she sallied

forth to retail her wrongs to a few of her special
cronies, and was wounded with the coolness with which
her explanations were received. Jack had evidently
the public sympathy on his side; indeed, Margery's
conduct was looked on as a grave breach of village
etiquette.

Evening came, and with it most of the merry-makers,
cheerful, solemn, or quarrelsome, according to the
amount of beer each had consumed during the day.
But no shabby figure in corduroys and clogs found its
way to the Gilly-f'ers; and at last, anxious and angry,
Margery went out to look for her husband.

As she crosssed the green, behold! there was Jack
outstretched beside the stocks, with his head resting on
the bench, sound asleep—so fast asleep, indeed, that he
did not hear his wife shouting in his ear, nor seem dis-
turbed when she shook and pommelled him.

Finding all her efforts useless, she drew herself up,
and looked at him with wrathful scorn. If some folks
could only see him now they would own that she had
been right to try to keep him out of harm's way. If
she had her way every one in the village should come
and see for theirselves the kind of a husband she had—
laying there dead drunk against the stocks, as in old
days a man would be clapped into fast enough for mis-
behaving same as him. It would serve him right to
pop him in now—give him a good lesson, it would, and

let the neighbours know his goings on. Margery had a good mind——

She stopped suddenly, and began pushing and hauling at Jack's prostrate form. She was a vigorous woman for her time of life, and soon got him into the requisite position. A momentary compunction struck her as she moved away after she had finished her task, and she looked back several times.

The old figure looked so forlorn propped up against the bench, the white head hanging forward, the feet, with their knitted socks of blue yarn and their huge clogs insecurely balanced on the toes, protruding stiffly from either hole. But she would not allow herself to be softened. It was for his good, after all, and he deserved a lesson.

It was quite dark when Jack came to himself, feeling cold and stiff and ill at ease. A lantern was flashing in his eyes, and quite a number of faces were bending over him.

"What's to do?" he murmured confusedly. "Wheer-iver have I got to?"

He felt the grass beneath his hands, and was astonished to find he could not move his legs.

"I've had a stroke, I doubt!" he said to himself, his consciousness returning with a sudden keen throb of anguish and fear. "I mun ha' had a stroke," he repeated aloud. "Wheer's our Margery? Wheeriver am I?"

"Nay, lad," said some one, "ye haven't had no stroke. Ye're i' th' stocks, that's wheer ye are, reet enough."

"It's your missus as has served ye a bit of a trick,"

chimed in another voice, and then there came a laugh. "Eh, she's a gradely one, is Margery o' Gilly-f'ers! She clapped ye into the stocks, owd lad, when ye was fuddled, and left ye your lone to get sober."

"Well, 'twas a shame," remarked another speaker. "If it hadn't ha' been for me I doubt she'd have left ye here for th' neet. I only wish I'd ha' lit on ye before, an' we sh'd ha' gotten ye out a bit sooner."

They had released him by this time and helped him to rise. Poor old Gilly-f'er Jack! He felt as if he were the victim of a nightmare, with the light flaring in his eyes, the crowd of faces surrounding him, one or two laughing, the others wearing a look of pity quite as humiliating to the independent old fellow. And— what was it they were saying?

"My missus—put me i' th' stocks!" he muttered after a moment or two, staring blankly from one to the other. "She—put me i' th' stocks! Our Margery, as has been wed to me this five-an'-thirty year! Did ye say she put me i' th' stocks?"

"Ah, Joe Whiteside's Tommy saw her—didn't ye, Tommy? He was frightened to tell us, he says. Eh, but ye should ha' told us, Tommy. Why, poor owd Jack theer might ha' been dead afore mornin'!"

Jack pulled himself together with a sort of shiver, and pushing through his friends, set off walking hurriedly in the opposite direction to the village.

"Howd on, owd chap! Yon's not the way home!" cried one of the men, running after him.

"I'm not goin' home," said Jack. "I'll niver go

home no more. Ye can tell her so. I'll niver set eyes on her again."

He would listen to no remonstrances, and, shaking off the hands which sought to detain him, struck out again, and presently disappeared into the darkness.

He walked on doggedly for hours, though his limbs shook and his head felt dizzy and queer, and was thoroughly exhausted when at last in the cold grey dawn he made out the undefined shape of a shed in a field near the road.

"I mun lay me down a bit," he said to himself, "or else I'll drop down. Eh, to think I should come to this—sleepin' i' th' fields same as a tramp!"

He thought of the warm feather-bed at home, and the pile of blankets, and the flannel-lined patchwork quilt. Margery no doubt was tucked up quite comfortably, while he was outside in the cold dew. Perhaps she thought he was still in the stocks. Very like she did, he mused, and a big sob rose up in his throat. Oh, that *she* should have served him so—Margery, his missus!

There was not much sleep for Jack, but he dozed a little from time to time, and rose up at last, aching in every limb. After pursuing his march for some hours he found himself in a big manufacturing town, through the streets of which he shuffled, jostled at every step by

the passers-by, and feeling puzzled and not a little
alarmed.

It was lucky for him that with all his timidity and
simplicity he retained a certain amount of shrewdness,
and did not manage his affairs so badly as might have
been expected, on the whole. He engaged a room in
a quiet back street, and after knocking about for a
day or two, till his little stock of money got low,
was fortunate enough to obtain employment—not very
remunerative employment, but still sufficient to pay for
his food and lodging and to keep him supplied with
"shag." He was so quiet and good-natured, so
regular in his goings and comings, and so easily
pleased, that the good people of the house grew quite
fond of him. He had his own place in a corner by the
fire in the little parlour behind the shop, and here of
an evening he would smoke a pipe with the master of
the house while the "missus" retired upstairs to put
the children to bed. It was long before Jack could get
out of the way of hastily pocketing his pipe and
assuming an air of elaborate unconsciousness when the
good woman reappeared. It seemed such a strange
thing that she did not "sauce" him for smoking; but
indeed so many things were strange to Jack nowadays,
that he lived in a state of bewilderment. That no one
should "barge" at him for making a clatter with his
clogs, or for getting his clothes dirty, or for spilling his

tea; that his pipe should be tolerated, and that he should be actually invited to partake of an occasional mild brew of whisky and water, were perpetual marvels to him. The presence of the children, too, of which there were half a dozen or so generally tumbling about on the floor, helped further to astonish and puzzle his poor old brain; yet, oddly enough, it was when they had retired for the night, and Jack and his host sat tranquilly smoking, that our friend felt least at ease. He would stare at the stolid face opposite to him as if wondering how it came to be there, and then take his pipe from between his lips and glance round the room with a sigh.

"Eh," he would say to himself, "it's quiet here! Eh, it's—it's awful quiet!"

Then he would think of the little kitchen at home, and of Margery's active figure bustling about, and of her sharp voice. It was more natural-like, all the same, and a man didn't feel so strange and lonesome. If only his missus hadn't served him such a trick? No man would stand that—and Jack's meditations generally ended in a glow of anger and resentment.

The months wore away; Christmas had come and gone, and spring had arrived, and one day it chanced that Jack on returning from work met a girl in the street selling wallflowers. The sight of the great basket full of brown and yellow and amber blossoms,

133

the familiar scent, the touch of the velvety bunches as she brushed past, were too much for him. He leaned for a moment against a lamp-post, trembling.

"Fine wallflowers, a penny a bunch!" shouted the girl, paying little heed to this tall grey old labourer.

She was now out of sight, and Jack, heaving a deep sigh, walked slowly homewards. So they were in season again! He wondered how the missus was getting on. She'd never be able to cut them, not she! And if she hired a man to do it, what would become of her profit? She'd have to get some one all the same, and Jack did not half like the idea of any outsider hacking at his wallflowers—they'd spoil the plants among them, most like. He himself had always been so careful never to break or injure them, to avoid bruising the roots, to economise the buds. All that evening he thought of his field of gilly-flowers and of the old life and of Margery. He felt a certain pity for Margery—*she'd* never make nothing out of them, *that* she wouldn't! Happen, by this time she was sorry enough for having "druv" her husband away from her. *She'd* never make no hand of they gilly-f'ers; it 'ud really be a'most worth a man's while to step up Thornleigh way and see how she was gettin' on.

That night he dreamt of his gilly-f'ers, and next day as he went to his work he still thought of them, and fancied he smelt them, and sometimes even stretched out his hand as though to take hold of them. And at last the gilly-f'ers drew him countrywards, and he found himself walking rapidly in the direction of his home. His face wore a very sheepish expression as he approached Thornleigh; the neighbours would laugh at him, he reckoned, and Margery—how would she receive him? He had not quite made up his mind as to what he should say to Margery, but he knew that he was very tired of being away from home. He approached his house by a circuitous route, not wishing to meet any of his former friends, and being most anxious to avoid the neighbourhood of the stocks. He insensibly quickened his pace when the familiar odour of the wallflowers first greeted his nostrils, and his heart was thumping, and his eyes full of tears, as he passed through the little gate and in at his door. A woman was standing in the kitchen superintending something in a small saucepan on the fire—not Margery, as the first glance told him; at the second, he recognised with some alarm the portly figure, red face, and squinting  eyes of a very different person—Mrs. Nancy Frith, who was char-woman, washerwoman, manager of *the* shop, on ordinary occasions, but whose real vocation lay in what she termed "nus-sin'." From the admin-istration of "cinder-tea" to a baby, to the adroit "chucking" away of a feather-pillow from under the head of a dying man to hasten his departure when his agony appeared unduly prolonged, there was no branch of her craft in which she was not an adept. Most of the infants of the village had begun life, and all the moribunds had become corpses, under her superintendence. Occasion-ally, indeed, the former had been unhandsome enough to upset her calculations and defraud her of her lawful dues; but the latter rarely disappointed her. From the moment when, fixing her swivel-eye upon their blanching countenances, she had first informed them they were "sadly warsening" to that in which—when the patients were tall and the stairs narrow—she had cheerfully recommended their removal to a room on the ground floor, it being "a dale o' trouble to get a coffin out o' winder," they had ever justified her confidence and submitted to her decrees.

Jack's heart sank as he saw her; and pausing abruptly, he thrust forward his shaggy head and inquired tremulously if the missus were ill.

"God bless us!" ejaculated Mrs. Frith. "It's never you, Jack Rutherford! Well, it's time ye come back to look arter your poor wife, as has been deein' all th' winter! Ye're nobbut just in time, too, for she's sinkin' fast. An' the way she've took on about you —it 'ud melt a stone, it would. Only a two-three minutes ago she says to me when she was choosin' th' sheet I've to wind her in, 'Eh, she says, 'to think as it won't be me as 'ull have th' layin' out o' my poor owd man! I've allus said as wan o' them sheets theer 'ud be for him, an' th' t'other for me;' she says, 'an' to think as it's me as has to go first, an' niver knowin' wheer he is, nor what's come to him! An' happen,' she says, 'it'll be th' Parish as 'ull lay him in's coffin, wi' nobbut some cotton rag or other to lap him in. Eh, she did take on."

137

Jack's jaw had dropped and his face had turned an ashy-grey colour.

"She's—she's deein'?" he asked, in an awe-stricken whisper.

"An' what else could ye expect?" responded Nancy, fixing him with one eye, while the other gazed steadily out of the window. "You goin' off an' leavin' her to fend for hersel', an' she a lone woman, an' gettin' on in years, an' frettin'—eh, she did fret! She never looked up arter ye left, an' comin' on Christmas she took to her bed, an' theer's she's been mostly iver since. Ah, ye'd best go in to her, ye'll not have her so long."

Jack staggered across the kitchen and opened the inner door, closing it after him, and standing for a moment, without speaking, just within the room where his wife lay.

She was very still, and her face looked strangely drawn and white as it rested on the pillow. She turned her head as he entered, and gazed at him fixedly.

Jack gave a queer little one-sided nod, and cleared his throat.

"Well, missus?" he said.

"Jack!" she exclaimed, with a faint cry. "I thought I was dreamin'. It's niver our Jack!"

"Ay," said he, approaching hastily, "I'm—I'm——" And then he broke off, and sat down suddenly on the bed, "Eh, missus!" he murmured under his breath, "eh, poor owd lass!"

Two great tears leaped out on his wrinkled cheeks; but Margery stretched out a feeble hand, and laughed a thin quavering laugh.

"So ye're back!" she said; "I'm pleased to see ye— eh, I am pleased. An' yet I doubt we wunnot be so long together. Doctor says I'm goin' a long road, Jack."

Jack looked at her, and the big babyish tears rolled slowly down his cheeks and fell with a splash on Margery's hand.

"I'll be a deal comfortabler now ye're come," went on the latter feebly. "Ye'll see to things, won't ye? An' theer'll be no need to have Nancy fidgetin' about, an' waitin' for the breath to go out of my body. Ye can get her to come to lay me out, ye know—I were talkin' to her about it, an' settlin' about coffin an' that. Ye might's well get Billy Rufford to make it—me an' his mother was awful thick while she lived, poor soul. He'd do't as well as any one, I reckon."

"Ah, happen he would," agreed Jack dolefully, but interested too.

"I've no such likin' for plain deal; it's awful common," resumed Margery; "but I *should* like pitch-pine. Eh, I've an awful fancy for pitch-pine—d'ye think Billy 'd make it o' pitch-pine, Jack?"

"I'll see as he does," quavered Jack, wiping his eyes with his coat-cuff.

"Thank ye," said his wife, meekly. "Eh, I'm glad ye're back, Jack—I'm glad to see ye', an' I'll be sorry to leave ye! Ye was allus a good man to me, Jack."

"She awful bad!" said the poor old fellow to himself, overwhelmed at this new tone. "Doctor's reet—she's goin'. She don't speak nor yet look like our Margery. She mun be goin' fast."

But he said nothing aloud, only sat there staring at her with woebegone eyes, and holding her thin hand in his.

Presently Nancy Frith appeared, carrying the posset which she had been concocting in the kitchen, and immediately flew at Jack for sitting on the bed.

"Just look at the way ye've messed all th' sheets wi' your dusty clothes! An' feather-bed all pushed o' wan side, an' your wife a'most smothered. Ye munna sit theer."

"Nay, he can bide," interrupted Margery, fretfully, "I can do wi' him; he's no need to move."

Jack shook his head afresh over this unusual tolerance, and Nancy fairly gasped. A further surprise awaited her, however, when Margery informed her peremptorily that she had no further need of her services, as her husband would "do for her" in future.

"He'll let ye know when I'm gone," she added tranquilly, "an' ye can look in, an' do all as is wanted then."

Mrs. Frith did not at all approve of this arrangement, but had no choice but to comply, and accordingly took herself off in some dudgeon. Then Margery heaved a sigh of deep satisfaction.

"Ye can see to me, can't ye?" she said. "Eh, but it's a comfort t'ave your own folks about ye again."

"I'll see to ye," said Jack, and then silence fell between the two. The old woman dozed a little, and her husband sat on the bed and looked at her, ejaculating, "Eh, missus!" occasionally, in a dolorous whisper.

It was quite dark when Margery spoke again, so suddenly as to startle him.

"I doubt I shouldn't ha' put ye i' th' stocks," she observed.

"I reckon ye did it for my good," returned Jack, huskily.

"Ah," assented Margery, "I meant it for your good, an' I niver meant to leave ye theer for th' neet. But happen I didn't ought to ha' done it. I'm glad as I can tell ye so. I've bethought mysel' many a time as happen I were a bit 'ard on ye sometimes—an' ye were awful patient."

"Nay," growled Jack through the darkness. "Theer was niver no call for patience. I didn't ax no better missus nor what ye've allus been. I were—reet enough. Have I to fetch a candle now?"

He stumbled out of the room and gave vent to his feelings in the kitchen, sobbing and rubbing his eyes as if he were seven years old instead of seventy.

For the next two or·three days he scarcely stirred from his wife's bedside, and his ministrations, clumsy and awkward as they were, seemed to be acceptable to the invalid. She quite revived as she directed and admonished him, and now and then there crept a shade of sharpness into her voice which filled Jack's heart with rapture. The mere fact of having some one to look after and keep in order seemed to give her a stronger grasp of life, and as the days passed, and the doctor saw that she was still holding out, he began to think that there might yet be a chance for the old woman. One day, when Jack was seating himself by the bedside according to his custom, after having tidied the room and given Margery her breakfast, she pulled back the checked curtain at the head of the bed, and looked at him sharply.

" Isn't gilly-f'ers ablow now?"

" Ah," said Jack, " a deal o' them."

" Well, just you go out an' cut 'em, then. We can't afford to let 'em go to waste. I wonder at ye, that I do!—an' doctor to pay, an' so much money goin' out."

" I were loth to leave ye," pleaded Jack.

"Well, I can do without ye, well enough," responded his wife, tartly.

Jack went to work without more ado, but, being uneasy in his mind, returned so often to inquire how Margery found hersel' now, and if she was pretty comfortable, that after the tenth visit or so she lost patience.

"Be off wi' ye," she cried, "an' don't come moiderin' me again. I'd rayther have your room nor your company, ye owd dunderhead."

Jack closed the door and went out again, chuckling and rubbing his hands.

"Owd dunderhead!" he repeated. "That sounds more like our Margery! Same as owd times, that is. I reckon she'll do now."

He whistled as he stooped over his gilly-f'ers, and often paused to laugh to himself and nod in the direction of the house, winking and looking very knowing.

"Owd dunderhead!" he would mutter from time to

time, in high glee. "Ah! I reckon she's turned th' corner."

His prophecy was realised, and in less than a week the doctor was amazed, on looking in, to find his patient sitting up in the bed "bunching gilly-f'ers," and rating her husband soundly.

AUNT JINNY

ALL Thornleigh was much excited when Mrs. Martha Billington came to live there. Her husband had been a native of the place, and was reported to have left her a nice little bit of money; and when she took up her abode at the Quarry Cottage, opposite " Rutherford's," the whole neighbourhood dropped in to make her acquaintance, and to condole with her, and to be regaled with the harrowing account of her gaffer's last end.

He had been a tailor by trade, and things had prospered fairly with him, and would have prospered more, had not the " sprees " in which he occasionally indulged caused him to neglect his business for weeks together. One of these sprees had terminated fatally. He had left his home and had not returned. Mrs. Billington loved to describe her uneasiness, her inquiries, her anxious search, and the anguish with which she had at last identified a body washed up on the shore yonder as that of her lost Richard. It was true he was *that* far gone that most people would have found it difficult to recognise him—Martha laid stress on this point—but she had at once identified his hair and his waistcoat; and the shoemaker last employed by him swore to the patches on his boots; and so she was enabled to draw his insurance money and to give him a handsome funeral.

The Rutherfords were, as has been said, her nearest neighbours, and curiously enough Joe Rutherford was

a widower. He was a big, shambling, thickheaded, soft hearted fellow, with "a rook o' little childer," whom he would have been altogether at a loss how to bring up had it not been for his Aunt Jinny. On the death of his wife, three years before, he had asked Aunt Jinny to keep house for him, and she had given up her work, said good-bye to the cousin with whom she lodged, and carried her "bits o' things" triumphantly down the lane to Joe's. The neighbours laughed a good deal, and wondered what hand an old maid " same as her 'ud make of all they little 'uns," and " how long it 'ud be before the baby followed its mother."

But Jinny had no misgivings : she sat down at once beside the cradle, and smiled her toothless smile at the sleeping infant, and informed the other children in a whisper that if they were careful not to disturb it she would make a po-tato-cake for tea. Thus was

Aunt Jinny's reign inaugurated, and a happy and pros-perous one it proved to be. Joe and the children were better " done for " indeed, the house cleaner, and the garden more orderly than in the time of the late Mrs. Rutherford, upon whom Thornleigh had been wont to look down as " a sickly poor cratur " at the best of times. Jinny was never happier than in the little patch of garden, and her roses and nasturtiums and sweet-peas were the admiration of the countryside. A lilac bush stood on one side of the little gate, and a red thorn-tree on the other, which made a brave show in spring. It was a pretty little place altogether, this tiny, flag-roofed, red cottage, perched on the very edge of the "delf," where gorse bloomed gaily in the clefts, and tall reeds and yellow irises grew in the water at the bottom. But eh! it was very small, Martha Billington said, and she wondered how Jinny was not moidered to death with all those children messing about in such a bit of a place; but she constantly made her way there all the same. Being a lone woman, it was natural that she should call upon Joe to help her whenever she wanted firewood chopped, or a shelf knocked up, or a door-handle screwed on; and being a matron of long standing who had "buried three of her own," it was equally natural that she should bestow a great deal of advice on old maid Jinny, who couldn't, as she frequently observed, "be expected to know much about the bringin' ups o' childer." Jinny didn't, as a rule, make "much count" of what Mrs. Billington said, though she was a little nettled when told that the baby was but a wummicky thing, and that Teddy would certainly get "nesh in his in'ards if she didn't give over stuffing him with traycle-butties."

She was seriously annoyed, however, when Joe took to quoting Mrs. Billington, and to stating with un-necessary emphasis that *she* really was a stirring woman now, and to "looking in" on the widow almost every evening to see if she wanted any odd jobs doin'.

No one was surprised when the banns were given out between Joseph Rutherford and Martha Billington; and Jinny put the best face she could on the matter, though she couldn't help takin' it rather 'ard o' Joe, and wondering whatever he could be thinkin' of to marry a woman ten year older than himself: she occasionally said fifteen, but that was in moments of extreme exasperation.

"An' what will ye do now, Jinny?" asked one of the neighbours commiseratingly on the eve of the wedding.

"Do?" said Jinny. "Why much same as I've allus done, I s'pose."

"An' how'll the new missus like that?" inquired the neighbour. "Ye'd happen better follow Mary to Upton. I reckon things 'll not be so comfortable for ye here."

Mary was the cousin with whom Jinny had formerly lived. She was a dressmaker by trade, and had recently left the village and "set up" with a widowed sister at Upton.

Aunt Jinny's face fell, and she began to rub her shrivelled hands together.

"Mary couldn't do wi' me now," she returned. "My sight's too bad for th' sewin', an' 'Liza an' me niver did get on so well. An' it 'ud seem strange to leave Thornleigh now. The childer 'ud happen fret, poor things.

They're used to me, ye see, an' I couldn't find it i' my
heart to leave them. Eh, I'll be reet enough. Joe 'ud
niver get on without me now, an' Mrs. Joe'll happen
find me useful. I doubt for all she's so stirrin', she
isn't such a terrible one for work as Joe thinks, an' she
won't care to be troubled wi' th' childer."

So Jinny, with the best grace she could muster, gave
up her place at the head of the table ; and the new
Mrs. Rutherford took possession of the teapot and
carved the Sunday beef, though she was kind enough to
allow her husband's aunt to cook it, and moreover to do
most of the scrubbing and cleaning, and to undertake
the family wash. As for the children, it was astonishing
with what confidence she abandoned them to the care
of the old maid ; though she took advantage of her
authority as step-mother to forbid treacle-butties, and
potato-cakes had become things of the past. But she
certainly did her duty by them in the matter of cuffs
and scoldings, and the little Rutherfords spent, in consequence, much of their time out of doors. Joe, too,
who appeared a little startled and uncomfortable at this
new state of things, went much oftener to the Upton
Arms than in former days, and Jinny grew silent and
depressed. There was not much love lost between her
and Mrs. Joe, and though she saved her niece-in-law
much trouble, the latter secretly longed to get her "out
o' th' road." Jinny, however, evinced no signs of wishing.

to depart, and Joe stoutly and indignantly resisted any of his wife's hints as to the desirability of inviting her to take up her abode elsewhere.

So things went on uncomfortably, and when the winter came Jinny was short-sighted enough to complicate matters by a sharp attack of rheumatic gout.

Certainly Mrs. Joe couldn't be expected to attend to her—Jinny herself saw that—and as the children were so young, and Joe at work all day, and as nobody had money to be throwing away on hired attendants, there was obviously nothing for it but for Aunt Jinny to go to hospital in "town." So poor Jinny—a mere bag of aching bones—was put into a cab, and drove off with Mrs. Joe beside her, and cried piteously under her wraps all the way. Mrs. Joe left her at the hospital and returned every week to see her, a sign of "feelin'" which touched Jinny and cheered her with the hope of better times in future. She grew better at last, though she was wretchedly weak, and it was doubtful if those poor distorted hands of hers would ever be fit for work again. Still, she was practically well, and one day triumphantly informed her niece-in-law that she was to be discharged in the following week.

"The childer'll be glad to see me, won't they?" she chuckled.

And then Mrs. Joe told her that Joe and she had

been thinking, and really it was very unfortunate, but they didn't see how they were to manage about her now.

Jinny sat up and gasped.

"Joe thinks, ye know," pursued her niece, "as it can't be expected as he can do wi' a sick body i' th' 'ouse. Times is bad, an' th' childer has but him to look to. There's th' expense to be thought of, ye know, an' who's to do for you?"

"Eh, I'd not want no doin' for," pleaded Jinny, big drops suddenly standing on her brow. "I—I could soon manage little jobs about th' 'ouse, same as I used, ye know—an' my mate's not much," she added wistfully. "I allus was a poor eater."

But Martha was firm. Any one could see for theirsel's as Jinny 'ud niver do a hand's turn again. Besides, Joe had said plain as he couldn't keep her, an' what was a body to do? The man was gaffer in's own house.

"Joe said he couldn't keep me?" repeated poor Aunt Jinny. "Eh, well happen he's reet. But what mun I do?—wheere mun I go?"

"Eh, theer's lots o' places for poor folk, now, wheer they're as comfortable as can be," returned Mrs. Joe. "Things isn't as they used to be, ye know. Why, yonder theer, at th' north side o' town, th' old folks has parties, an' tea-drinkin's, an' a lovely yard to walk in——"

"D'ye mean at. the Union?" interrupted Jinny, clasping her poor twisted hands appealingly. "Eh, Martha, will Joe let me go theer? Martha, Martha, mun I go theer? Eh, Martha, let me dee at home! I'll soon dee—I'll niver ax for nowt; but don't say I have to go yonder!"

But of course she did have to go yonder: there was nothing else for it. And as for returning to Thornleigh for a week or two first, as poor Jinny desperately suggested, who was goin' to be at th' expense o' shiftin' her back'ards and for'ards? Martha wanted to know. Jinny was too weak and too old and too ill to withstand her, and a few days later found her at that Gehenna of the respectable poor, the workhouse. Everything was very neat and clean and orderly; her food was plentiful and good of its kind; and Jinny was still feeble enough to be sent at once to the infirmary, where she found her bed fairly comfortable and her neighbours on either side quiet and well-spoken. But as she lay there staring blankly at the white-washed wall opposite, or drew her head under the clothes to weep at her ease, she said to herself that it was a dreadful place, and wished with all the ardour of her poor old heart that she could die. But she didn't die; she got better instead. And by-and-bye the little dainties which had been considered necessary for her were cut off, and soon she was allowed to get up and sit beside her bed, instead of lying in it. After Christmas, they said, she would be well enough to leave the Infirmary and go into "the House." Jinny listened blankly—after Christmas what did anything matter? She was to spend her Christmas in the Union and that was enough for her.

Some of the other paupers, old-stagers contented with their lot, talked gleefully of the fine doings she might expect at Christmas; they always had a party, they said, and the ladies came and played and sang for them, and there was a Christmas Tree. And then Jinny thought of how she used to put toys and sweeties at the foot of the children's beds at home, and turned her face to the wall. Ladies visited the wards sometimes, chatting to the patients, and cheering them with little presents of tea, and snuff, and lozenges; and one day a young girl came in and sang for them.

Aunt Jinny sat very still, listening; her hands folded in her lap, her dim eyes gazing at the glaring white wall—ay, and through it, and beyond the squalid streets and the miles of stony road at Thornleigh, and her youth and green fields and friendly faces. The young voice paused, and then rang out afresh; and all at once Jinny became old and miserable again. It was the Christmas Hymn which resounded through the room now—the Christmas Hymn, and here she was in the Workhouse! Rising, she uttered a hoarse cry, and stretching out her lean arms, fell sideways on her bed, her whole form writhing convulsively. The singing ceased abruptly, the nurse hurried down the ward, the patients craned their necks to see what was the matter with the woman—was she in a fit? But Jinny was only sobbing.

Then the singer came to her, and took her hand, and spoke kinds words to her; and Jinny grew calmer, and presently explained that the Christmas Hymn had upset her terrible, and that she couldn't, couldn't, not if it was ever so, make up her mind to th' thought o' spendin' Christmas i' th' Union.

"If it weren't for th' thought o' Christmas I think I could welly resign mysel'," said Jinny, looking up, while big tears coursed down her wrinkled nose. "I welly think I could. But, eh! to be here at Christmas —I *can't* say th' will o' th' Lord be done!"

"And if you could go away for Christmas, do you really think you would mind being here less, afterwards?" asked the young lady.

"That I would!" returned Jinny, with conviction. "I could bear mysel' better. You know, miss—I can't tell you how 'tis, but it seems as if I couldn't niver hold up my head again arter spending Christmas i' th' workhouse."

The girl was young and perhaps not very wise; but her heart was soft, and her purse was full, and so when no one was looking she slipped a half-sovereign into Jinny's hand.

"Now you can go away for Christmas," she said.

Who could describe Aunt Jinny's joy, and the

feelings with which on Christmas Eve she found herself
hobbling along the road to Thornleigh. It was only
two miles from Upton station, and Jinny had preferred
to walk, and to spend the few shillings which remained
to her after paying her railway fare and her cab
"across town," in presents for the children.

There were oranges and sugar-sticks in her bundle,
and a doll for Polly and a trumpet for Teddy; she had
even managed to buy a necktie for Joe Rutherford
and a bright-coloured handkerchief for Martha. Thus
laden, she thought she could not fail to be welcome—
she had winked to herself indeed, and rejoiced in her
own cunning, when she had chosen the handkerchief.
Martha would certainly be civil after such a present
as *that*; and as for the others, bless their hearts! she
knew they would be glad to see her. It was true that
she had wondered and fretted a good deal "yonder,"
because Joe never came to see her, but now she told
herself that it wasn't to be expected. He would be
glad to see her now—this was more to the point. She
pictured the slow smile which would creep over his
face. He would surely cry out, "Why, it's niver Aunt
Jinny!" and then the children would dance round her
and clap their hands. How surprised they would all
be! Jinny chuckled to herself as she thought of it.
That was almost the best part of it. They would all
be at tea most likely when she got there, and she would

tap at the door and say, "A Merry Christmas to
you!" and then what a pushing back of chairs, what a
fuss and scampering there would be! Martha might
look a bit sour at first—very like she would—but
Jinny would make haste to present her handkerchief,
and would whisper in her ear "I've not comed for
long," and so *she* would begin to be pleasant. Perhaps
Joe might say as he didn't see why Jinny need go back
to the Union—she wasn't not to say sickly now. But
there! it was best not to think o' that. She would
stay over the New Year at any rate.

It was difficult to walk along the road very fast, for
the trodden snow was slippery and Jinny's limbs were
stiff and feeble; and the oranges would keep slipping
out of her bundle, and rolling just out of arm's length.
It would soon be dark, and still she had a good way to
go; but she thought of the bright lights in Thornleigh
yonder, and the warm fire, and the children's happy
faces, and trotted on, still smiling to herself.

She had just picked up an orange for the seventh
time, and re-knotted her bundle and straightened her
back, when a portly figure suddenly rounded the corner
of the road, and paused, starting back at sight of
her.

"Why, Martha!" cried Jinny, colouring faintly, and
stretching out her hand.

"Aunt Jinny, it's niver you!" ejaculated Mrs.

Rutherford. "Whativer brings ye here? An' wheer on earth are ye goin'?"

"I were goin' home," quavered Jinny, making great haste to fumble in her pocket for Martha's handkerchief. "I'm not comed for long—just for Christmas, Martha, I couldn't stop in the Union at Christmas-time, ye know. A lady gave me ten shillings for my ticket an' that, an' I've some little presents here——"

She shook out the handkerchief and diffidently proffered it to Martha. "I thought happen you might find this come in for yersel'," she added tremulously.

Martha took it and turned it over, and then tendered it back to her, with an odd look on her face.

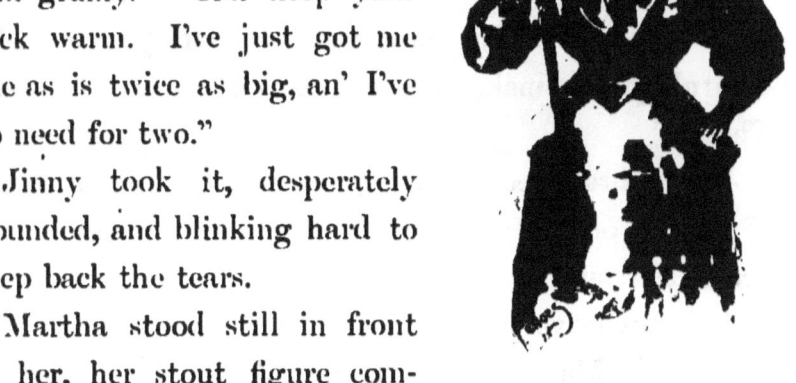

"You'd best keep it," she said gruffly. "It'll keep your neck warm. I've just got me one as is twice as big, an' I've no need for two."

Jinny took it, desperately wounded, and blinking hard to keep back the tears.

Martha stood still in front of her, her stout figure completely blocking up the path; something in her very attitude, as well as the expression of her stolid face, making the poor old woman's heart turn sick within her with a new, awful fear.

"I'll not stop long, Martha," she whimpered.

"Ye'll not stop at all," returned Mrs. Rutherford. "Ye munna think o' goin' to our place. We couldn't do with ye. Why, woman, what should ye come to shame Joe an' th' childer for—them as ye think so much of? What 'ud all the neighbours say if they knowed their aunt was i' th' Union?"

"An' wheer do they think I've bin all this time?" asked Jinny, her tears suddenly ceasing, though she trembled like an aspen leaf.

"I' your grave!" said Martha, setting her arms akimbo and looking fiercely defiant. "I towd 'em ye was dead—theer! An' I towd Joe ye was dead an' th' childer. An' Joe's bin weerin' a black band on 's 'at for ye all th' winter—an' he'd be fit to kill me if he knowed. So I'm not goin' to let ye come to Thornleigh to make mischief between man an' wife. Theer!"

Jinny's brain reeled, and she sank down, a very heap of misery, on the snowy roadside, feebly trying to push her niece from her, as she bent over her.

"I'll not leave ye till I see ye on your way back to town," said Martha. "'Ark now, Jinny Rutherford, it 'ud be the worst day's work ye did i' your life if you come between Joe an' me. An' what's more, he'd niver 'old up his head again if it was said as ye come straight to his house fro' th' Union. Theer, now! It'll be no kindness to him if ye do, I tell ye."

"Very well, then," moaned poor Jinny. "Ye needn't trouble yersel', Martha; I'll not go nigh him."

She struggled to her feet with the aid of Mrs. Rutherford, and held out her little bundle.

"'These here bits o' things—I'd like th' childer to 'ave 'em. The doll's for Polly, an' the trumpet's for Teddy, an' theer's marbles for th' other lads, an' a few sugar-sticks an' things. Ye might tell 'em as "—with a great gulp—"as Feyther Christmas sent 'em. An' theer's a necktie here as I got for Joe. Will ye give it him?"

Martha promised, looking rather sheepish as she took possession of poor Jinny's little gifts. There still remained the handkerchief which Jinny, after contemplating it for a moment and observing with great dignity that she wouldn't trouble Martha with *that*, flung over the hedge.

Then she wrapped her shawl more closely about her, and turned round.

"Good arternoon!" she said, hobbling off slowly in the direction whence she had come.

Martha watched her for a few minutes, and, finding she did not pause or turn her head, heaved a deep sigh of relief and betook herself homewards.

Jinny walked on, sobbing as she went, and occasionally lurching against the hedge in her weakness and despair. It was growing dark now, and her sight was blurred with tears, so she made many false steps, and at last stood stock still, feeling she had neither strength nor spirit to advance further.

Why need she hurry, after all? What great speed was required for a journey which was to end in the workhouse.

Oh, the cruelty of it—the injustice—to force her to go there, and then to be ashamed of her! And Martha had told every one she was dead—Joe had been wearing a black hat-band for her!

Such poor vitality as Jinny possessed tingled within her with indignation.

She felt outraged and humiliated. How was it that if Joe had thought her dead, he had made no effort to go to her funeral? Martha had probably "put him off" in some way, but all the same Jinny felt this slight to her imaginary corpse acutely. Where did they suppose she was buried, and how? Was it possible folks thought she had been buried by the Parish? The blood swept over her face at the idea. It was the crowning ignominy, the bitterest drop in all her cup of gall. And yet this was what she must surely come to. She would never leave that living tomb to which she was about to return until she was carried out for her pauper funeral.

Yonder stood Thornleigh Church dimly defined against the murky sky; yonder lay her father and mother and all her people; and *she* was to go back to die in the Union, to be buried by the Parish!

She started forward, clenching her hands.

"That I won't!" she cried, and she began feebly to drag herself towards Thornleigh—a certain desperate determination shaping itself in her mind the while. She had promised not to go back there to live, but she would go back there to die. She would creep under cover of the darkness to Rutherford's corner

of the churchyard, and there she would lay her down. She had heard that people who laid them down in the snow slept never to wake again—well, it was better than going back to die in th' Union. And when the people found her in the morning, lying with her own folks, they would see that she had not been buried by the Parish; and Joe, she knew, would make sure that she was carried to her long home decent.

It seemed a long journey, and it was certainly a painful one, but Jinny reached her goal at last, and sank down on her mother's grave. She had a right to be there at least—no one could turn her away. This was her place—with the dead. Oh, the snow was cold, and Jinny was numb and weary! But she summoned up all her courage, and composed her weary limbs, and folded her arms on her breast. She would say her prayers now.

"Here I lay me down to sleep," she began, using the little formula which she had repeated every night since that far-away childhood of hers. But the words would not come right, and she could not rouse herself sufficiently to recall them.

"Here I lay me . . . . here I lay me down to sleep," she repeated aloud, drowsily, and then she began to see bright colours, and to feel very comfortable—so comfortable that she was not a little indignant presently when she became aware that somebody was shouting in her ear and endeavouring to raise her.

After a long blank interval she found herself, to her immense astonishment, seated before a blazing fire in the Canon's kitchen; the Canon's housekeeper was chafing her feet, the Canon himself rubbing her hands; while opposite to her, with open mouth, and eyes goggling almost out of his head, was her nephew, Joe Rutherford, himself.

" Joe ! " she ejaculated faintly.

" It is her," said Joe, clapping his hands ecstatically.
" It's hersel'—it's Aunt Jinny. How she comes 'ere
beats me—but here she is, an' that's enough ! How
are ye, Aunt Jinny ? Eh, I'm fain to see ye, but my
head's that fuzzy, I welly think I mun be dreamin'."

The honest fellow, who had been half laughing and
half whimpering during this speech, here made a clutch
at Jinny's hand, pumped it vigorously up and down, and
burst out crying.

But when Jinny presently told her story, feebly and
by slow degrees, his countenance changed ; and when
the Canon, seeing that his indignation excited and
further exhausted the old woman, sent him out of the
room, he went straight home and thumped Martha.

His feelings imperatively demanded an outlet of some
kind, and this appeared to him equally suitable and
satisfactory. Wife-beating was practically unknown at
Thornleigh, but on this occasion Joe certainly did correct
his spouse in the manner above-mentioned, and it must
be owned that she deserved it.

Jinny lay between life and death for several days, the
strain and shock and subsequent chill proving almost
too much for her. The Canon had duly lectured her
for having courted death as she had done, but there
were times when he thought to himself that death
would be the easiest solution of Jinny's difficulties.

She was happy enough now in the little "spare room" at the Presbytery; but when she got well she could not, of course, stay there; and though Joe insisted that she must return to his house, Martha would probably make her life miserable if she did. There seemed no way out of it—it was almost to be hoped that Jinny would die.

The puzzle was solved, however, in the most extraordinary and unexpected fashion by the discovery of no less a person than Mr. Richard Billington himself.

His last "spree" had, it seemed, proved too much for a brain at no time one of the strongest, and he had passed the ten months which had elapsed since his disappearance in the county asylum, where, in Christmas week, he was seen and recognised by an honest farmer and his wife on visiting their lunatic son.

They described him as alive and well, and—except for a rooted conviction that he was the Emperor of Germany, and an unfortunate disposition to bite every one who refused to pay him homage—as sane, they said, as they were. The Canon set off at once to make sure there was no mistake, being accompanied by Martha, who was obliged to acknowledge the identity of her husband. How his boots and his waistcoat came to be worn by another man was a mystery which was never cleared up. But there he was, an incontrovertible fact; so Martha had to pay back the insurance money, and to say good-bye to Joe, and to become Mrs. Billington again. She left Thornleigh and returned to the town, where she supported herself by washing, and was much honoured and respected to the end of her days, as became a woman with a grievance. It was not merely the fact of being a grass-widow with a husband in a lunatic asylum which called forth the sympathy of her acquaintances—"but to think that she spent all that money in buryin' a man as was no kin to her?"—eh, she had seen trouble, poor soul!

Joe bore up wonderful, Thornleigh said, and the children were out of their wits with joy. As for Aunt Jinny, she postponed her dying to an indefinite period, and went back to keep house for them again. And though she was stiff and rheumatic still, it was wonderful how much work she managed to get through. Soon the episode of Joe's second marriage was remembered only as a bad dream; but Jinny never laid her down "o' neets" without breathing a prayer "for all poor folks as has no home o' their own."

ON THE OTHER SIDE
OF THE WALL

ON THE OTHER SIDE
OF THE WALL

THE park wall of Thornleigh Hall forms a background to the village, and the wood on the other side is a very paradise to the children. In the long spring evenings a dozen or so may often be seen scaling this boundary wall, and with a careful twist of their little persons— for there still remain some fragments of broken glass on the coping—and a flourish of arms and legs, disappearing one by one. Then begin birds-nesting, and fern-collecting, and flower-gathering, and a score of other delights, all the sweeter because forbidden. If a keeper comes in sight, or a gardener, or a member of "the family," there is a sudden stampede, and in two minutes—lo and behold! nothing is to be heard or seen but a group of urchins innocently playing marbles in the village street.

On principle I am of course opposed to anything which savours of trespassing, but still I must own that if I were a little village boy I should find it hard to keep out of Thornleigh woods; indeed, even as it is, I fear I spend many an hour in their enticing shade which should be more profitably employed. Birds-nesting never did possess any charms for me, and I like to see the ferns and flowers growing where

they list better than gathering or transplanting them; but certain emotions and enthu-siasms wake within me as I stroll under these branches which make me tolerate and even sympathise with little freebooters in corduroys. I confess that my heart beats as I prowl round "likely" bushes, and of a sudden, with a shriek and a flapping of wings, a blackbird or a thrush flies almost into my face. There is her nest, and there the tempting eggs warm from her breast—one can understand the itching of schoolboy fingers to lay hold of them. In the entrance of a disused rabbit-hole, low down in a mossy bank I know of, a pair of robins built once, and many a time did I kneel in a rather muddy ditch to peer into their curious dwelling-place, the little palpitating mother sitting on her eggs the while.

Ay, this is magic ground; there is witchery in woodland sights and sounds and scents. Those rows of daffodils that "take the winds of March with beauty" —how shall an urchin refrain from gathering an armful of them—is not "a boy's will the wind's will?" But to me the long undulating golden lines are lovelier when unbroken. There is abundance of gold here when the year is young—here a patch of primroses, there a very plain of celandine, golden moss on ground and tree-trunk, a golden mist of opening leaf-buds, and golden sunshine over all. Ah! that little water-hen in yonder pool, how she dives at sight of me! Her wee simpletons of chicks paddle distractedly over the spot where she has disappeared, dipping their heads in imitation of her, but leaving the rest of their minute

egg-shaped bodies in full view. A group of wild
cherry-trees stand near this pool, and in the spring its
waters are white with fallen blossoms. Late spring or
early summer is the time to see Thornleigh woods in
their glory; when their green livery is at its leafiest,
and the undergrowth of rhododendrons is ablaze with
blossom; the white and pink and crimson of the
cultivated varieties contrasting with the more plentiful
lilac of the wild ones. Some of these have spread to be
very trees, with twisted branches, and a thickness of
trunk under their shining green which testify to their
age; yet year after year the blossoms cover them, fresh
and young and sweet—laughing children climbing
round the old stock.

Up this beaten path to the right one can get a
glimpse of the Hall. Not a very imposing building
perhaps, with its low frontal and irregular architecture
—a wing here, a tower there, windows at uneven levels,
the very stones, where the ivy lets them be visible, of
every conceivable shape and size. But if these stones
could cry out, what a tale would they tell! Many a
curious drama has been enacted within those old walls,
and many a strange vicissitude have they witnessed!
Certain of the records treasured in the Squire's study
yonder tell us mournful and curious histories of the
struggles it cost those stout old ancestors of his to
cleave to their traditions. As Catholics and Jacobites,

one may imagine how many storms they weathered, how often ruin must have stared them in the face, banished as they were, and imprisoned, and fined. But they held on their way still, clinging to their ancient manor while their people clung to them. To this day

the bond between squire and tenant is almost unique in its strength. The Thornleigh people are shrewd, and rugged, and hard-headed enough, the last in the world to be accused of truckling to the higher powers; but they love and support their squire because he belongs to them, and they understand each other. Their fathers did the same by his father, and the bond can be traced backward for many generations. Perhaps no stronger proof of the harmony of relations between landlord and people can be cited than the fact that there are few leases on the property, most of the tenants holding their land by virtue of a verbal agreement.

Thornleigh possesses its own Local Board, and levies its own rates, ay, and discusses them hotly—the Squire arguing from the chair, the members growling forth their opinions as they sit round the board; everything is on a free and friendly footing at these meetings—a very good footing, which is more than is ever likely to be afforded by their roads.

But now it is time to say a word or two about the lord of the manor himself. "A fine old English gentleman" indeed, but not of the hackneyed type; none of your drinking, brawling, swearing ruffians, who are frequently cited to us as samples of "the old school." There is never a foul word to be found on his lips, or an ungenerous thought in his heart. He will uphold his dignity on principle, and is tenacious of family traditions; but he would not think it beneath him to shake hands or exchange jests, on occasion, with the poorest of his labourers, and he can do a day's work still with the best of them.

Watching the tall burly figure, upright still in spite of its seventy odd years, looking into the kindly open face, hearing the cheery voice, one realises the magnetism of his influence over a people, staunch and sturdy and "jannock" as himself.

See him now with coat and waistcoat open, and axe on shoulder; he has been thinning out the undergrowth of elders in the woods. Indeed, as the people say, "Squire's allus agate at summat." All country pursuits are delightful to him. He is, of course, a sportsman from the crown of his fine old white head to the soles of his thick shooting-boots, and an adept in woodcraft of every description, and is, besides, a clever gardener and carpenter. He has indeed a carpenter's "shop" of his own, where on wet days he spends hours, working with as much zest and earnestness as though his living depended on it. The real joiner's shop, yonder near the farm-yard, is also a favourite resort of his, and hardly a day passes that he does not visit the queer old brace of carpenters at work there. These can hardly be included among the "hangers-on" of whom there are so many at Thornleigh. When an old workman begins, as he says, to "weer away," and is no longer equal to much exertion, he becomes what is called "a handy man," and is kept in heart and in pocket by the daily allotment of nominal tasks. These are sometimes a little difficult to find; but the self-respect of the poor old fellows who accomplish them is not wounded as would be the case if they were offered money which they had not earned. So they paint gates—leisurely and without too much attention to detail—and salt bacon, and occasionally trap rats. One old gentleman indeed became such an adept in the destruction of this class of vermin that no one ever called him anything but " Billy Rat." I fancy that at last he himself would have found it difficult to recall his "gradely name." A queer, wizened-up, knowing-looking little fellow was Billy, regarded by the village children with wonder

and awe, for his method of exterminating rats was mysterious, not to say uncanny. He did not trap them, or hunt them with " tarriers," or poison them, at least not with ordinary rat-poison. He just " laid down" an innocent-looking preparation of his own, and the rats disappeared. After Billy's dealings with them never a rat was seen, or heard, or, stranger still, smelt about the place. But he guarded his secret jealously, and would reveal it to no one. It eventually died with him, and the plague of rats has now returned to Thornleigh. The old carpenters before alluded to, however, are still equal to their full day's work, and receive their full day's wage; though the youngest of the pair is seventy and the eldest the patriarch of the village. The latter, Joseph Birch, is a tall lean old man with marked features and a curiously pallid complexion. He is almost blind, and to conceal this fact, wears his hat tilted over his *worst* eye, with a rakish air at variance with his rather serious face and manner. His defective sight is a sore point with him, and he is much put out if any one is ill-advised enough to notice it; while he hastens to cover by laborious explanations any chance awkwardness on his own part which would seem to betray it. " I were just bethinkin' mysel' o' summat, an' didn't chance to see ye," he remarks, when he has perhaps violently cannoned against you; and then, staring in the direction from which your voice proceeds, he will tell you that " you're not lookin' so very well to-day," and ask " How's that ? " Having by these precautions recovered the ground lost by his false step, he shambles on again, and, when he thinks you are out of sight, puts out his hand cautiously and feels his way by the wall.

" One comfort is," he observed, once in a moment of unusual confidence, " Squire's never found out as there were aught amiss." The little fiction of the perfect clearness of Joseph's vision is indeed kept up by the master with quite as much perseverance as the man.

" Do you see ? " the Squire says, pointing out some defect, or describing some wished-for alteration in the job on hand; and Joseph puts his head on one side and scratches his jaw meditatively, and remarks that he has noticed that himself, or that indeed he has unbethought himself about · it, and doesn't seem to fancy the looks of it as it stands.

He is a first-rate carpenter in spite of his affliction, and his work, planned and measured as it is entirely by touch, is neat and solid.

His brother craftsman, the youngster of seventy already alluded to, is looked on by his chief, and most of their fellow labourers, with a kind of half-pitying contempt. His youth, to begin with, is against him, and besides, he is a new-comer and· comparatively a stranger, having only worked on the estate a matter of thirty year or so. Why, many in the place can remember the day he came tramping from Cheshire with a bundle under his arm, looking for work ! That alone, it is owned by even the friendliest of his neighbours, would make a body think different. It is true, he comes of decent stock, it is said, and was even then a clever artisan ; but "there's allus a kind of a feelin', ye know, when ye don't know a man's folks, an' wheer he's comed from, an' that." So Robert is tolerated, and patronised, and occasionally put in his place ; and bears it all with exceeding good humour. He is a small, slight, wiry man, bald and white and toothless, and to the full as deaf as Joseph is blind. Joseph is very kind and magnanimous about his subordinate's infirmity, though sometimes he is obliged to comment on it ; and he whistles to Robert when he wishes to attract his attention, and makes elaborate and extraordinary gestures to illustrate his meaning in a compassionate and condescending manner.

"You poor lad can't hear, ye know," says Joseph ; and Robert's little blue eyes look up twinkling, and presently he asks respectfully, "Did ye see the little brad-awl anywhere ? "

A few years ago, another great crony of the Squire's was alive. Old Johnny was perhaps more devoted to his master than any one else on the estate, but then, as he said, he had good reason to set store by Squire. He was a handsome, stalwart, white-haired old fellow, who had begun life as a cow-man, and who to the end of his career was consulted by all the neighbourhood on knotty points connected with live stock. On fine afternoons he might be seen enthroned on a big stone in the farm-

yard, munching his baggin' or smoking his pipe, and giving audience to his clients—a picturesque figure in his old-fashioned garments: long-tailed coat, blue knitted stockings, clogs and breeches. There was a story about those breeches which Johnnie would tell occasionally, after a due amount of persuasion.

"They breeches! Ah, I set a dale o' store by they breeches—an' well I may."

"They seem a good stout pair," one of the listeners would perhaps suggest, perfectly aware that this was not the reason Johnnie valued them, but anxious to humour the old fellow by leading up to the point gradually.

"Ah, they are that. Joe Orrell, as made 'em, has allus good stuff—I will say it—stuff as 'ull welly weer for iver, an' look well to the last. Ah, he's a pretty fair tailor is Joe, though 't isn't so much his part o' the business as I think th' most on. Theer's others as has had a hand i' th' tailorin' o' these here breeches, I can tell ye. Ye wouldn't happen think as Squire had aught to say to them, would ye now?"

Here his little audience would smile and nudge each other: the story was coming now. "Ah," Johnnie would continue, singling out with his eye any member of the group to whom the tale was genuinely new, "ye wouldn't think it—but theer! This is how it were. I were comin' whoam latish, one neet, a two-three year

184

ago now. I'd been up yonder at Granny Gibson's seein'
a pig as she had as were sick. It were at th' last, poor
beast, an' I towd her she'd best send for butcher to fetch
it away. An' Granny took it very well—she's rale
religious, is Granny. 'Th' will o' th' A'mighty be done!'
says she, 'an' arter all th' Lord's good. It might ha'
been one o' th' lads!' Well, as I were saying, I were
comin' whoam latish, an' takin' a short cut through the
wood, when all of a sudden I heerd summat creepin'
arter me—sticks breakin', ye know, an' every now an'
then a sound same as a footstep. I turned me round
an' looked, an' theer was nowt as I could see, so then
on I went, an' the creepin' an' crackin' went on too.

"'Well,' thinks I, 'this is strange!' an' I didn't feel
not to say comfortable, for all the boggart tales as
iver I'd heerd come into my head, an' I'd half a mind
to turn back an' not go through th' owd buryin' ground
as lays theer, ye know, just at th' corner o' the wood.
Folks as pass by theer o' neets tell queer tales. But if
I'd gone back I'd ha' had to pass yon thing, whativer
it were, as were followin' me, so that stopped me
again.

"Well, I gave another look round. It were gettin'
reet dark, but I thought I saw a shape o' some mak'
under th' trees. That was enough! Off I set, runnin'
as 'ard as iver my poor owd legs 'ud take me, an' if th'
thing didn't begin runnin' too! I dursn't look round

again, but I could 'ear it plain. Well, I knowed theer weren't no use i' my thinkin' I could run faster nor it, but I bethought mysel' all at once o' th' owd cross i' th' middle o' th' burial-ground, an' says I, 'If I can but reach yon, no boggart as iver walked can come next or nigh me.' Theer it were, an' theer was I sweatin' to get to it, an' yon were th' boggart comin' arter me fast. I clomb up the mound (wi' th' boggart behind me) an' catched howd o' th' cross, an' if th' big stone top doesn't give way! Down I comes faster nor I got up, with it a-top o' me, an' my two legs broke!'"

Pause, during which Johnnie looked triumphantly round, enjoying the sensation. "Well," he would resume presently, "I were knocked a bit silly at first, as ye may think, but when I come to, theer was a leet flashin' i' my eyes, an' Squire an' Bob Prescott bendin' over me.

"'Eh, Johnnie, Johnnie,' says Bob, 'howiver could I guess it were you? Why didn't ye holler?' says he; 'in all the fifty year as I've been keeper 'ere, I niver see such a piece o' work as this!'

"'Wheer's th' boggart?' groans I, as well as I could, for th' pain o' my legs was awful.

"'Did you take Bob for a boggart?' says Squire. An' 'Eh man!' says Bob, 'I took ye for wan o' they raskilly poachers!' an' he were fair cryin', poor owd lad, thinkin' he'd done for me.

"'Come, Bob,' says Squire, 'pull yourself together; get some one to help us to carry this poor fellow home,' he says. 'His legs are broken, and must be seen to at once.'

"'Eh, Squire don't ye trouble yourself,' says I. 'I'm done for! I am that!'

"'Keep up your heart, old chap,' says Squire; an' he sits down aside o' me wi' 's pipe in 's mouth, an' looks at me. 'Keep up your heart, old chap; ye're pretty tough, you know, Johnnie. We'll have you about again in no time.'

"Well, arter a bit, a lot o' lads comes fro' th' village, an' our missus wi' them, cryin' fit to break her 'eart.

"'Come, come, Molly,' says Squire, 'he's not dead yet.' ''T won't be long first, though,' says th' lads as were shiftin' me. Eh, I thought I sh'd ha died upo' th' road; but when they geet me home an' laid me o' th' bed, Squire come an' stood aside o' me. 'Now,' says he, 'there isn't any doctor at hand, Johnnie, so I'm going to do what I can for you myself.'

"'It's very good of you, I'm sure, Squire,' says I, groanin' awful, 'but I doubt it's scarce worth your while —I reckon I mun dee.'

"'Nonsense,' said Squire, 'a broken leg or two never killed a man yet.' (Ah, that's what he said—'a broken leg or two!') 'Now, let's see,' says he, 'these breeches

187

'll have to come off, and they're such a beautiful tight fit—you are such a dandy, Johnnie, you know—we can't pull them off.'

"'Eh, lord!' says I, all of a shake at th' notion, 'don't go for to do that, Squire! Cut 'em—cut 'em t' pieces, if ye like—I'll niver want 'em no more?'

"'Johnnie, don't be wasteful,' says Squire, as cool as a cucumber. 'A good, stout, serviceable pair of breeches! Of course you'll want them again, and you'll be very sorry if they're spoilt.'

"Then he whips out his knife, an' looks across at th' missus. 'Don't be frightened, Molly,' says he, 'I'll do no damage.'

"An' if ye'll believe me, he slit down the seams, that careful, ye know, stitch by stitch, an' me hollerin' all the time, as 't weren't no use his takin' all that trouble, an' 't were nobbut a wooden suit as I wanted now—meanin' the coffin, ye know. Squire niver tak's no notice, an' goes on just same, an' when he'd done he hands over th' breeches to our missus. 'There now,' he says, 'ye can sew 'em up again, an' they'll be ready for the gaffer when he gets about.'

"Well, he'd done it as clever, th' owd woman said, as she could ha' done hersel'. Niver so much as a thread o' th' stuff cut. Then he hunts up laths, an' handkerchers, an' that, an' sets my legs for me. An' here they

are, reet enough, breeches an' legs too—as good as new,
I may say!"

Here Johnnie used to stretch out his nether-limbs
and gaze at them affectionately, ejaculating half to
himself "Squire's handiwork!"

There was universal regret when the quaint old figure
disappeared from our midst. Johnnie had been repair-
ing a certain fence, which he was anxious that the Squire
should find in good condition on his return to the Hall
after a short absence, and worked so eagerly that he
caught a chill. For two or three days he lingered,
dozing a good deal, and sometimes wandering, talking chiefly of his work, as these simple, toilful old
folk do.

"He fancies he's about yon fence still," whispered his
daughter, between her tears. And Johnnie went on
drowsily chopping wood, and hammering nails, gesticu-
lating with his big feeble hands, and muttering half-
articulate comments on his fancied labour. "Theer we
are—reet . . . Yon's too short, I doubt . . . A plague
upon those nails . . . Theer, now we're gettin' it."
And then he fell to plucking at the sheet, and was
silent—silent so long and so absolutely that his children,
grey-haired men and women some of them, and his
children's children, who had gathered round his bed,
looked at each other inquiringly.

"He's gone," said one at last. But not yet. His

eyes opened once more and travelled round slowly, and a smile crept over his face.

"I mun see an' get a' fettled up afore Squire comes home," he said, and then closed his eyes with a little sigh—and went Home himself.

LITTLE PAUPERS

ALL the chubby rosy little people who may be seen flocking to Thornleigh school are not natives of the place: there is a floating population of " boarders-out " —workhouse children billeted here and there in the village by " the Union." They are principally girls, for the thrifty Thornleigh matrons value the "hand's turn" they can get out of them occasionally quite as much as " the bit o' money" that they receive for their keep. But now and then a farmer or a cow-keeper finds a pauper lad " come in useful " for driving a milk-cart, or cleaning shippons, or performing odd jobs that it seems a pity to " pay out wage " for. It is only fair to say that as a rule these children are exceedingly well fed and well treated ; but nevertheless there is, and always will be, a certain distinction made between little Isaac and little Ishmael. Thus, while the child of the house is free to play by the roadside after school, the workhouse child must come in, and scrub a floor or clean the pots and pans : here and there their meals, though the same in quality as those of the rest of the family, are partaken of at a separate table, and at Christmas-time, when there is dancing and tea-drinking and merry-making all over the place, the little boarders-out are left behind. The Canon usually gave a consolation party for the "pauperines" as he called them. *There* was joy and triumph! The proud sisters had perforce to stay at home, and the little Cinderellas went to the party; and the Canon poured out their tea, and stuffed them with cakes, and told them stories, and played the piano for them to dance to; altogether there was no end to the rapture and the glory.

Jack Davis was a workhouse boy who had been brought up at Thornleigh from the age of two, his master, Farmer Morris, calculating that he would be big enough to work by the time his companion pauper, a lad of eight, was too old to be paid for by the Union. Some people laughed at this foresight of Farmer Morris's, and reckoned the brat would do more damage than his keep was worth long before any work could be got out of him.

But as time passed the village folk changed their tune, for not only did his master find him useful, but nearly every man, woman, and child in the place contrived to get "a hand's turn" out of Jack. Now the little round-faced, fair-haired lad would be seen driving in the cows for Mr. Waring, now running to the shop for Granny

Gibson, or to the pump with Polly Birch's kettle, or to some distant field with Joe Rutherford's baggin'; and

now toiling along the dusty road which led to Upton, bent almost double under the weight of an overflowing

clothes-basket, while its rightful owner sauntered
leisurely in the rear, gossiping with a friend.

The women rewarded him with a "There's a good
lad!" the men with an inarticulate grunt at the end of
his journey; and little Jack would look up brightly, and
wipe his brow with his jacket sleeve and start off at a
brisk pace to see if he was wanted anywhere else. There
never was such a good-natured, good-humoured, "willing"
urchin as Jack Davis—everybody liked him and everybody made a drudge of him. The "little beast of
burden," as the Canon called him, was so ubiquitous,
so obliging, so prompt, so blithe, that it was almost
impossible to avoid taking advantage of his anxiety to
make himself useful.

"Who is to fetch that parcel of books from the
station?" the priest would ask, perhaps.

"Oh, Jack Davis said he would go after school," the
mistress would reply as a matter of course.

"Did you, Jack? I thought my housekeeper was
sending you in the opposite direction for some eggs?"

Then Jack would stand up, extending his little red
paw as a sign that he wished to speak: his blue eyes
jumping out of his head with eagerness.

"Please, Canon, I can easy do both afore milkin' time!"

"Milking time!" echoed the Canon with his kindly
laugh. "I had forgotten Mr. Waring's cows. Poor
little beast of burden!"

196

He knew there was nothing which offended Jack more deeply than to refuse his proffered services, or, indeed, to neglect to ask for them when required. Once Jack had cried for a week because the Canon had omitted to tell him he was setting out on a journey at five o'clock in the morning, and the child was too late to carry his bag to the station. On the next occasion Jack "made sure" of him by sitting on the doorstep of the Presbytery all night.

With this general amiability, Jack was so diligent at his lessons, so punctual in coming to church, so pious, so honest, so painstaking, that sometimes the Canon would shake his head over his excessive goodness.

"It *can't* last," he would say. "I know it can't last. He will either die or take to 'coortin'!'"

But years went by, and the Union left off paying for Jack, and Mr. Morris began to pay *him* the very smallest sum he could decently offer him, and Jack went on working for him and everybody else, and grew a little taller and a good deal broader; and by-and-by a sort of flaxen fluff appeared on his upper lip. He would very soon be a man; and yet so far the alternatives dreaded by the Canon seemed equally remote.

One Sunday afternoon, however, the Canon happened to be strolling along a lane in the neighbourhood of the village, when he came suddenly face to face with

Jack and—a young lady. A very smart young lady, though up to the last two years she had been a pauperine. She was now servant at one of the farms at Upton, and in the receipt of sufficiently high wages to enable her to wear a locket with a blue stone in it, and a hat with a pink feather. I am not quite sure if she was leaning on Jack's arm, or Jack on hers, but arm-in-arm they were, and apparently on most affectionate terms.

The Canon stood stock-still in the middle of the path and gave them one of his terrible looks.

"John Davis," said the Canon, "and Margaret Lunt, what is the meaning of this?"

John Davis stood motionless, his eyes goggling, and his face turning from red to purple and from purple to white. Margaret Lunt sobbed, and choked, and coughed, and then putting her finger and thumb in her mouth took out a large bull's-eye.

"Please Canon, he's my young man," she observed, diffidently.

"*Indeed!*" said the Canon, and then he turned to Jack, but found it difficult to preserve his gravity as he descried the outline of what was evidently a companion bull's-eye clearly defined in the youth's cheek. Steadying his voice, he resumed with becoming severity: "John, I am surprised at you! How often have you heard me speak about the folly—and more than folly—of such behaviour as this? Do you not know that I always set my face against this—this senseless love-making which can never come to anything?"

"Please, Canon," returned Jack, speaking somewhat inarticulately, partly on account of emotion and partly on account of the bull's-eye—"please Canon, we was—we was comin' to you."

"Coming to me? What for?"

Jack nudged Maggie, who, as a rule, was more glib with her tongue than he; but on this occasion she was so much overwhelmed with bashfulness that she could only hang her head, till the Canon observed that the pink feather was fastened at the back of her hat with a very large and crooked brass pin.

"Well?" he asked, after a pause.

Maggie nudged Jack and murmured indignantly, "Go on—can't ye?"

"Canon," said Jack, "I take it rayther 'ard that ye should sauce us for what's nobbut reet. Maggie an' me's made up our minds to get wed, an' we was just comin' to ax ye if ye'd put us up next Sunday—the banns, ye know——"

Here the would-be bridegroom came to a sudden stop owing to the bull's-eye unexpectedly tumbling out of his mouth: he looked down at it as it rolled along the path, and then put his foot on it, much as if it had been a beetle.

"Banns!" said the Canon, struggling with a violent inclination to laugh, "and bull's-eyes! How old are you, Jack?"

"Very near nineteen," responded Jack with somewhat sulky dignity. "An' as for they bull's-eyes, I dunnot mak' so much count o' them. It's Maggie as was that set on my tryin' one——"

"'The woman gave me . . . and I did eat,'" muttered the Canon, and he laughed outright. "The old story! So you are fond of bull's-eyes, Maggie? There, don't be afraid—hold up your head. I don't at all find fault with the bull's-eyes—I only object to the banns. How old are *you*, Maggie?"

"I'm turned sixteen," whispered Maggie, faintly.

"Oh, children, children!" said the Canon laughing again, but presently composing himself, he sat down on the bank that edged the road, and looked at Jack, who somehow did not seem so crestfallen as he expected.

"What are you going to marry on?" he asked more seriously. "How do you propose to live? You both only earn a few shillings a week besides your board, and when Maggie gives up her place she will of course lose that; and even if Mr. Morris continues to employ you—which I doubt—I am quite sure he will not give you wages enough to keep a wife on. No—no, it is absurd for either of you to think of marriage for several

years to come. And meanwhile there must be no talk
of keeping company—understand that."

"Canon," said Jack much wounded, but still dignified,
"it's just because I do understand that I were comin'
to ye. I'd niver have gone for to say a word to
Maggie without I had it all settled. Her an' me's
goin' to live in town when we're wed. I've the promise
of a job down at th' docks—an' good wage they give
too—an' I've seen a room as 'll just suit us. An' we's
do very well. Why should we wait? She's no one,
an' I've no one? If ye won't do the job yoursel' we can
get married at Upton. But I niver thought," added
Jack, with tears starting to his eyes—"I niver thought
as it 'ud be any one but our own Canon as 'ud——'
He paused, too much moved to continue.

The Canon was a little overcome himself, for he was
very fond of Jack, and besides being sorry to part with
him, he could not but see that this was a foolish business and would probably end in misery. The mere
thought of these youthful simpletons exchanging their
healthy happy country home for a room in some slum
near the docks was in itself a source of anxiety. And
then marriage before the bridegroom was nineteen—
beginning life "on the promise of a job!"—it was
deplorable! Nevertheless, in spite of everything he
could urge, Jack stuck to his point. Maggie and he
would take their chance; but get wed they would, and if

Canon wouldn't shout them next Sunday they would go to Upton.

"You are a couple of geese," said the Canon, getting off the bank at last; "but if any one is to marry you, it shall be myself."

"Shouted" they accordingly were on the appointed day, to the intense amusement of Thornleigh, which was unanimous in voting them "a pair of noddies." As neither 'of them had any relations that they knew of, nobody gave them anything except good advice. Of that they received enough and to spare, though the sum and substance of it all might have been condensed into the one famous word addressed by Mr. Punch to people in their situation. But they would—and they did, though presently Thornleigh, growing irate at their pigheadedness, said some severe things and uttered gloomy prophecies; Farmer Waring going so far as to tell Jack that he needn't come looking for help there when he and his wife found themsel's beggars.

"I'll clem first!" cried Jack with an angry flash in his eyes: it was the only time he lost his temper. Up to this he had received advice, remonstrances, and reprimands with imperturbable good-humour, but this remark "cut him a bit," as he subsequently observed.

All the same, on his wedding morning he drove up Farmer Waring's cows for him as usual, and filled Granny Gibson's kettle, and fed Mrs. Birch's pigs; and

then he changed his coat and went to fetch Maggie
to church. Maggie had expended her last remaining
shillings on a lace collar and a pair of flesh-coloured
silk gloves, which had to be peeled off with great
difficulty when the ceremony was about to begin. Jack
wore his rather threadbare Sunday clothes; he could
not afford to make any difference in his attire, for,
though he had been saving for several months before
he spoke to Maggie, his little capital was sadly diminished by the time he had purchased "the ring," and
paid for the hire of a room, and the few "sticks" of
furniture that were absolutely indispensable.

Nevertheless, as they stood at the altar rails together
the Canon thought he had never seen so radiant a pair;
and when they finally walked off arm-in-arm he smiled
and sighed together.

"Poor little beast of burden!" he said, "I wonder if
he realises the weight of the load he has taken on his
shoulders this time! But, after all, they have youth,
and hope, and health, and love. . . . . God bless my
little paupers!"

He watched them as they descended the church steps
and walked down the path; Maggie's head nodding, and
the skirt of her dress giving a little kick-up at the back
at every step. There was no giggling crowd waiting at
the lych-gate to deluge them with rice; nobody had
time or inclination to assist at this insignificant wedding;

no carriage was in attendance to convey them home according to Thornleigh custom—even if you only live

fifty yards away from the church it is the proper thing to drive to and from your wedding; no substantial meal was spread for them, no jocular guests gathered round, no health-drinking anticipated. Jack had some slices of bread and meat in a handkerchief, and Maggie had gooseberries in a paper bag;

and thus provided they set off to spend their holiday in the fields.

Jack was to "start work" on the morrow, and this was·to be their last day in the country, so they were determined to make the most of it.

It was beautiful summer weather: larks were singing overhead and butterflies flashing through the air; and there were cuckoo flowers in the grass, and marsh marigolds and "water-creases" and fat-stemmed blue forgetme-nots in the ditches. Once a big bumble-bee came booming and blundering past in such a hurry that he

nearly flew into Maggie's face; and she was frightened
and clung to Jack with a little scream.

"What's to do, *Mrs. Davis?*" said Jack, which sally
they both considered so exquisitely funny that they
stood still and laughed till the cows and horses grazing
in distant fields raised astonished heads, and looked at
them. Then they walked on sedately, Maggie resting
her left hand on Jack's arm, and smiling complacently
down at it every now and then: she had not resumed
her gloves, partly because she was hot, and partly because she was economical, but chiefly because she could
not see her wedding-ring clearly through the silk.

After threading many fields, and pausing to rest
themselves on a gate, they reached a range of sand-
hills bordering the sea-shore, and came to a stand-still
beneath the steepest mound.

" I mind," said Maggie, with a half-sigh of sentimental
reminiscence, "how I used to roll down this hill when I
was a child."

"Would ye like a roll now?" said Jack; "I'll shove
ye off from th' top."

"Eh, lad, how can ye talk such nonsense," replied
Maggie bridling; "for shame of ye!"

Thereupon Jack, composing his features, explained
that he had only been joking; and they climbed the hill
with much sliding and laughing and screaming from the
bride, whose arm was nearly dislocated by her husband

in his strenuous efforts to haul her along. Finally they reached the top and sat down, panting and laughing still; and when they recovered their breath they ate their dinner. Jack called Maggie "Missus" throughout this meal, and Maggie assumed pretty little airs of matronly importance. But presently they got tired of being dignified and began to try who could throw the gooseberry-skins farthest down the hill. By-and-by a big steamer was visible on the distant horizon, and Jack explained all about it to Maggie; then a white-sailed schooner hove in sight, which he also pointed out— calling it a brig by-the-by. In the far, far distance a forest of masts were defined against the clear sky— clear, save for the light cloud of smoke which hung over them and the adjacent town.

"Yon's the docks," cried Jack, nudging Maggie; "and nigh to them's home, lass!"

"Home," echoed Maggie gazing at the masts, and the smoke, and the distant roofs and chimneys with eager, ignorant eyes.

There was a delicious little breeze lurking somewhere near the top of that sand-hill, which went rustling through the star-grass every now and then, bending it into blue-green ripples, refreshing to look at; but the sun was hot enough to please Jack and Maggie, and there was a little patch of wild thyme just beneath their feet which sent up new fragrance every time they pressed it. The tide was in, and gulls were floating on the edge of the water, sometimes rising high above their heads with shrill screams and flappings of silver wings.

So the day wore away, and at last the great pageant of sunset was enacted for these happy pauper children as they sat poised. in mid-air upon their glittering throne of sand; and as they watched the golden sky and the golden waters, they felt themselves rich enough. And when the sun disappeared, and all the landscape was bathed in a mellow after-glow, they went hand-in-hand together down the hill and into the wide world.

HERE AND THERE

THERE has been a certain appearance of gloom over-
hanging the village during the last few days: the
wheelwright, handsome, genial Robert Whitgrave, died
on Sunday, and was carried to his "long home" yesterday. Poor Robert—no one ever thought he would go
off like that. It is true he was "getting into years
pretty well," and had grown-up children and half-a-
dozen or so of grandchildren; but he was hale and
hearty still, and could do a day's work with the
youngest. On Sunday, just as he was smoking a quiet
pipe in the garden before "cleaning him" for church,
he fell down in an apoplectic fit and never spoke
again.

"It was a mercy," sobbed his wife through her tears,
"that he hadn't time to put on his best suit. 'T
'ud ha' bin ruined for sure, for he fell reet again th'
pigsty."

The Thornleigh folk are not sentimental, as has been
before stated, and see no incongruity in a widow's

consoling herself with such reflections as these, even in
the first keenness of her sorrow, but the sorrow is none
the less genuine for its undercurrent of thrift. Thrift,
indeed, so oddly associated with grief among these good
plain-speaking village mourners, that sometimes it leads
to results which almost take one's breath away. I
remember once paying a visit of condolence to a poor
woman who had lost her two sons under peculiarly sad
circumstances within a few months of each other. After
many lamentations on her part, and expressions of
sympathy on mine, I sought to change the conversation,
and by way of raising Mrs. Wick's spirits began to praise
her tidy parlour, which, indeed, with its raddled floor,
polished furniture, and wealth of antimacassars and
china, was the picture of what a cottage parlour
should be.

"That is new, isn't it, Mrs. Wick ?" I said, pointing
to a large mat on the hearth, very neatly made of strips
of cloth fastened on canvas.

"Yes, ma'am, our Lizzie made it."

"It is very nice indeed. Where did she get all those
bits of cloth ? I suppose she begged the tailor for some
odds and ends."

"Eh, dear no, ma'am," returned Mrs. Wick, raising
the corner of her apron to her eyes, "it's the lads'
clothes, ma'am. Ye see we couldn't make up our minds
to part with them, an' it seemed a pity to let 'em

go to waste, so our *Lizzie* she took and made them into that, and it looks very well—now, doesn't it?"

The wheelwright's yard is desolate enough to-day, with no bustling figure moving about it, no cheerful clinking and hammering sounding from the shed; and within, a doleful party are gathered round the fire. Grief is still too new to permit poor Robert's womankind to set about their ordinary occupations, as they sit shaking their heads and looking gloomily at each other, while they recall various traits of the departed. The widow and her daughters sit at the  table, the children of one of the latter perched awe-stricken on a bench in a corner; while "Granny" Whitgrave, Robert's mother, a prodigiously old woman, is in possesion of a chintz-covered arm-chair in the ingle-nook. The younger members of the family receive the visitor after the first words of welcome with mournful and embarrassed silence, but Granny starts off, in a

quavering, piping voice, with garrulous lamentations
and touching reminiscences; relating often and emphatically how poor Bob used to come in of an evenin' an'
say, "'Granny' (he allus called me Granny), 'tak' a sup
o' gin, do. It'll do ye good,' he'd say. Ah! he was
that thoughtful—th' best son as a body could have.
'Tak' a drop o' gin,' he'd say, he would." And so on,
and so on till the new-made widow breaks in with a well-
meant endeavour to cheer the old lady by inquiring,
"Who'd ever think as poor Robert 'ud be took before
her? We was all expectin' her to go—indeed we knew
very well that she couldn't last so long, and to think
that arter all he was took first."

Here a fresh diversion is caused by the youngest of
the children sliding off the bench in the corner and
toddling up to its mother, laying a curly head in her
lap, and peering up shyly.

"Eh, ye'll niver guess what this lad's been playin' all
the morning," says the mother, stroking his curls
fondly. "What d'ye think? Burying his grandpa!"

The urchin laughs roguishly, and, mother, aunts, and
grandmother smile too—even the great-grandmother
uttering a shrill cackle from her corner.

"Ah! ye wouldn't believe it," pursues the mother,
sinking her voice, and winking towards me, "but theer
he dug a little hole so nice i' th' garden, and fetched a
little stone—that was th' coffin, ye know—'Now, pop

214

him in!' he says." She laughs this time, and stoops, beaming with modest pride, to kiss the child. They are all laughing in the house of mourning when I leave it, even the widow in spite of her heaving bosom and swollen eyes.

A few doors lower down I make a visit of another kind. A young couple live here, newcomers from the south of England, whose first child arrived on the very day of poor Robert Whitgrave's death. "Very unlucky," the neighbours told the young mother. She has not been much noticed up to this, being considered a "parvenu" and treated with the reserve which Thornleigh metes out to such. But when the poor thing was understood to be "near her time," and to be feeling lonesome and down-hearted in consequence, a few kind creatures felt it was but their duty to go and cheer her up a bit. So they dropped in, one by one, and told her she looked real bad, and it would be a mercy if she ever got over it. "Nobody ever lived in *that* house," they added; "the two last as had it died arter a few months, an' quite young women too—ah, just about her age they were. Eh, dear! it was a sad thing when young women went—an' leavin' children behind—eh, it was cruel! Sometimes, though, the baby went along o' the mother—particklerly if it were a first child; an' happen in the long run that it was the best thing as it could do—poor little thing! What could a man do,

ye know, as was left like that wi' a child to do for?
Well, it was to be 'oped as Mrs. Summers 'ud get on
all right, but, poor soul, it was no wonder she felt
nervous an' frightened. Did she hear that dog youlin'
last night? A strange dog it were. Some people
said, ye know, as it wasn't for good when a strange dog
came youlin' through the village—it was for a death,
ye know, so the sayin' went—but there was no believin'
such tales as them. But Mrs.
Polly Birch (Will Birch's Polly)
she minded how once, when she
was a lass, a strange dog—a kind
of a black and white greyhound
it were—coom i' th' night to their
place, and run youlin' round the house
three times, an' then run off, an' her
mother had said, 'It's for a death, I doubt,' an' sure
enough not more nor a two-three weeks arter a
letter coom wi' a big black edge on it to say as
her sister were dead. Ah! well, now Mrs. Summers
must keep her heart up, an' hope for the best. Did
she never hear no noises o' nights—nor see anythin'
queer? Well it was to be 'oped it *was* only mice, or
happen rats—though rats was nasty things enough in a
house; sometimes if a body was ill or that, they got
that bold they'd run over the bed, they would—aye,
an' bite a person's toes; but still, rats were but rats

arter all. But Margaret Lupton, the last as died i' th' house, she used to walk a lot up an' down this very room—aye an' stand for hours at yon gate when her breathin' was bad—she went off suddent at the end. There *were* people in the village as said poor Margaret was walkin' still—an' of a moonlight night some o' th' neighbours could often see somethin' as plain as plain standin' by the gate, an' some thought it were a calf, an' some a pony, an' some said it looked like a woman's figure; but if ye went up to it, ye'd find there was nowt to be seen. But people did get talkin' so foolish, an' Mrs. Summers had no need to be afeared. She must cheer up now, an' niver go for to cry; why, that was the very worst thing for her, an' th' little 'un as was on the road—every one knew that. An' they'd look in again arter a bit to cheer her up—ah! they would—for it was to be expected as she'd feel anxious an' low-spirited, poor soul."

These comforting assurances did not, however, exhilarate Mrs. Summers as much as might have been expected, and in fact it was not till her trouble was over and she could feast her eyes on her fine healthy little son that she at all regained her spirits.

She is sitting up in bed to-day, and able to laugh at her fears.

"I never got a bit of comfort out of my husband, though," she says; "he did nothing but joke an' make fun o' me. 'What 'ud spirits come back for?' he'd say; 'haven't they room enough in the other world? If they're well off, they won't want to come back; an' if they're not, they won't get a chance.' But he's very good to me. Every spare minute that he can find he comes runnin' home to see if I want anything."

It is lucky for poor Mrs. Summers that such is the case, for the neighbours, finding that no catastrophe has happened, and that they are not called on to comfort a disconsolate widower, have, after one state call to inspect the baby and assure the mother that it was not half the size of the ordinary run of Thornleigh infants, relapsed into their stately aloofness. But Mrs. Summers has got her baby to pet and gaze at and wonder over—wee fingers to curl round hers, tiny feet to hold in her hand, a small soft face in which to discover marvellous likenesses and beauties. Let the neighbours stop away if they like, her baby is "company" enough for her.

Next door to this house, where a little life has so recently begun, another little life, the life of a child, is rapidly ebbing away. Poor Gracie, not yet twelve, and dying of consumption! I remember her such a merry rosy little maiden, always tiny, but so bright, so full of life. It makes one sad to see her lying thus quietly in her narrow bed, soon to be exchanged for one narrower still; but she calls up a smile at sight of me, and beckons with her small wasted hand.

"She wants you to go close to her, ma'am," says the woman who looks after her (Gracie is a "pauperine"); "she can't speak above a whisper. She wants to tell you something."

I approach, and bend over the little creature, catching the faint words with difficulty: "Mrs. Francis —did ye hear as Canon has given me a grave?"

"Eh, she's so pleased!" puts in her foster-mother, smiling too, almost as radiantly as Gracie herself. "She was in such a way, ye know, thinkin' she'd have to be buried by the parish. These Union childer, ye know, when anything happens them, they generally fetches them away, and poor Gracie was frettin' so about it. But Canon, when he heard of it, came and said: 'No, no,

Gracie, we won't let them take you away; we'll find room for ye here,' he says; 'I'll make ye a present of a grave.'"

"Yes," says little Gracie, nodding feebly, "that's what he said, 'I'll make ye a present of a grave.' An' will ye come an' look at me when I'm laid out, Mrs. Francis?"

I promise, and Gracie smiles again with entire satisfaction.

"I'll pray for ye as soon as I get to heaven," she whispers after a moment, closing her eyes.

"Ah, I think they'll be tired hearin' about Thornleigh when Gracie gets up yonder," puts in the woman. "I dunno who she isn't goin' to pray for. Canon, an' Squire, an' the young ladies, an' Mrs. Francis——"

"An' childer'," interpolates Gracie.

"Aye, she says to me this mornin', 'I'll ask God to bless Mrs. Francis's childer' one o' the first things,' for she thinks such a dale o' them. Well, then there's—I don't know who there isn't——"

"Mother's leg," suggests Gracie, opening her eyes a very little.

"Oh yes, my leg—ye see, Mrs. Francis, it's always been a bit stiff like since I hurt it in the winter; but Gracie says she's goin' to settle about *that* when she sees Almighty God."

She pauses to jerk away a tear or two, and continues:

"Ah, she's settled everything—haven't ye, Gracie?
She's give away her doll, an' her new boots, an' her
clothes, an' her Prayer-book. Our Nanny's to have that,
'Mind ye're careful of it now,' she says quite sharp when
she give it her. She set a dale o' store by her Prayer-
book, poor little soul——"

"It's yonder on the cupboard," interrupts the child.
"Show it to Mrs. Francis."

I duly inspect and admire this treasure, its former
proprietress being particularly anxious I should observe
that it has gilt edges and a clasp; and then the little
dark head, which has been eagerly raised, falls back on
the pillow again with a sigh.

"I only hope as Nanny will use it well!"

"Ah," says the foster-mother, following me to the
door, "ye'll never see her alive again, Mrs. Francis.
She's goin' fast—'a question of hours,' doctor says this
mornin'. She was listening to him, an' when he'd gone
she says, 'Well, mother, happen ye'll be havin' a good
rest to-night'—I have to be up an' down a good bit
with her o' nights, ye know—'an' I'll be havin' a good
rest too,' says she, an' she laughs. Afraid? Eh, dear
no, ma'am. She's longing to go. 'It 'll be a good job
when I'm gone,' says she this mornin', 'for I'm a dale o'
trouble, an' it'll be lovely up theer. I reckon the
Almighty 'll take me to-day, an' you must have a good
sleep,' she says."

221

Here the kind-hearted woman, who is truly attached to her little charge, suddenly bursts out sobbing, and re-enters the house with her apron to her eyes.

I pursue my way more soberly after this, for the recollection of Gracie's tran- quil smile brings a cer- tain dimness to one's eyes, and a choking sensation to one's throat. After gazing at that quiet little figure, and stooping to catch that weak voice, it almost jars on one to see the troops of bois- terous young- sters playing in the mud,

and to listen to their whooping and laughter. This sunburnt well-grown lassie is just about Gracie's age:

I can hardly bear to look at her, though she has always been a favourite of mine. "Curly," she used to be called, in allusion to her thick crop of yellow locks, which curled so tight that when one pulled out one at hazard it sprang back into place again the instant it was loosed. These curls were rather a trial to their owner, because, though prodigiously thick, they were not long, and one day, when she was a very little girl, she cut them all off and buried them in the garden, having been told by a waggish friend that this was the way to make them grow.

My next visit is one of business: the village shoemaker has sent in his account, and as I am passing I may as well "settle" it. A very curious document is this yearly bill of his—he never will send it in oftener than once a year—the items being set down in a way which would puzzle the uninitiated :

	s.	d.
Soling and heeling son's boots .	2	6
Heeling and toe-capping daughter's .	2	9
Daughter's repaired . . .	1	6
New laced boots—son . . .	13	6
Your buttoned boots soled . .	3	9

And so on for a column or two.

In the next house there is also question of a bill, the doctor having recently sent in his account for medical attendance on the family during an exceptionally severe winter. The children have all been ill, and the mother "down" for weeks; medicine is included, and altogether the charge seems to an outsider reasonable enough, but I have to listen to many lamentations. I am told, indeed, that when the master opened it he nearly fainted, and when his wife saw it she fainted right off, and then her sister came in and *she* fainted, and they took it over the way to Aunt Maggie, and *she* fainted; it was a terrible piece of business altogether. Doctors have not always an easy time of it in Thornleigh. To begin with, the patients' relations have an irritating way of supplementing their prescriptions with nostrums of their own; an exceedingly delicate infant will be dosed with cinder tea, or stuffed with bread and milk, because "it seems, ye know, to be always cravin'" —the poor child, in all probability, suffering from violent indigestion. A man threatened with acute inflammation will be given a stiff glass of spirits to "warm his in'ards," or to "cut the phlegm." Then the question of remuneration is nearly always a vexed one, especially if, in spite of the doctor's utmost care and skill, the patient chances to die in his hands. Thus, when Polly Birch's child, having been taken out of its bed and carried across the road to a neighbour's, with the measles "thick on it," unfortunately succumbed, it was thought very sharp practice on the part of Dr. ——

to charge anything for his six visits. An old woman I knew once, who had been a martyr to asthma and chronic "brown-titus" for the last twenty years of her life, was at length induced by a friend to call in a doctor, and was mightily indignant because he failed to cure her.

She was sitting propped up with pillows when I last saw her, feebly endeavouring to sew a black band on the hat which her husband was to wear at her funeral, and occasionally glancing round to make sure that her winding-sheet, which had been, in accordance with her injunctions, put to "air" by the fire, was not scorching. She had evidently given up all hope of herself, but made use of such breath as remained to her to inveigh against the doctor and his bill.

"'Two pound ten, Mrs. Francis! An' the time he's been coming—an' the bottles an' bottles of stuff as I've drunk—an' here I am, deein'!'"

Opposite the shoemaker's live a couple of washerwomen —mother and daughter—the daughter white-haired and wrinkled, the mother inconceivably old, bent almost double, and totally deaf.

"Coom in," screams Kitty, who, from the constant  endeavour to make her parent hear, has grown accustomed to raise her voice on all occasions to a startling pitch, "coom in, ma'am, an' sit ye down. Mother!" giving the old lady a playful push with one powerful arm and propping her up with the other, as she totters under the impetus. "Here's Mrs. Francis coom to see ye. Eh, she've been bad this last week, Mrs. Francis, she have. I thought she were done for on Monday."

Old Margery, catching the drift of the conversation from the expression of her daughter's face, mumbles forth a lengthy history of various distressing symptoms, entering into minute and rather appalling details with obvious pride and joy, while Kitty puts in a word now and then to endorse these statements, and listens to the most harrowing particulars with every appearance of satisfaction.

"She do, ma'am. Ah! ye wouldn't believe what my

mother goes through. Eh dear! 'Kitty,' says she last neet, 'my inside's just same us a band o' music.' I told Canon that, an' says he, 'Wind instruments, Kitty, I s'pose.' Eh! he is foonny, is Canon. Wait till ye see my mother's leg, Mrs. Francis, you wouldn't raly think it could be so bad. Ye've been up to th' Hall, 'ave ye?"—as I hastily interposed to change she subject—"an' how's Squire? Ah! Squire's my favour*ite*, an' allus was, though Mr. Humphrey an' Mr. Edward is nice gen'lmen, too. Eh, there is but a few o' them left now—nobbut three lads an' two wenches. Miss Monica, as died last year in London, she were the youngest o' th' fam'ly, an' she was gone sixty. But eh! Squire allus was my favour*ite*. Ye'll have been seein' sick 'ere in village, I doubt. Poor Robert Whitgrave! he were carried off sudden—an's owd mother left. She's th' owdest i' th' village, nobbut mother 'ere. I reckon they'll be next, they two owd bodies—mother'll go first, I shouldn't wonder."

Here Margery, judging from her daughter's smiling face that something pleasant is going forward, smiles too and rubs her shrivelled hands together.

"Mrs. Summers is getting on nicely," I observe.

"Ah! so I believe" (drily). "Ye'll 'ave seen Mrs. Joe Morris. Eh! ye haven't bin yet. Eh-h-h! well now, raly! Ah! ye're goin' on theer now. Well, good afternoon. Coom again soon."

Mrs. Joe Morris is a bride, and should have been called on before. She does not come from this part of the world, and as Joe did his courting rather hurriedly, being anxious to get the business over before harvest-time, Thornleigh has hardly even yet had leisure to discuss her.

It was a very great wedding to be sure; all the Thornleigh folk who were present were mightily impressed. The bride, though she would never see forty-five again, was attired in white satin, and her father, a publican of some standing and anxious to prove himself well versed in the customs of polite society, appeared in full evening dress. " Eh, it was gradely," the village people said. Half a column of the " Fashionable Intelligence" of the paper published weekly in the little town where the bride's parents live was devoted to this wedding; and it was really very fine reading, quite equal to a paragraph in a Society journal. " Ornaments, pearls. . . . . The bride pronounced the solemn vow in scarcely audible tones, the bridegroom in firm and manly accents." Honest old Joe indeed saw no reason why his " Oi wull" should not be heard and understood by every one present, or, for that matter, within a radius of half a mile or so.

I hear his firm and manly accents presently, as I pass his farmyard, resounding even above the hum and clatter of the threshing machine; and as I stand on the

neatly raddled doorstep I hear the bride's tones
(exceedingly audible now) objurgating somebody who
had omitted to "sneck the door."

My knock, however, produces instant silence; there
is a good deal of running backwards and forwards, and
whispering; and after a few minutes a servant appears,
who ushers me into the best parlour, and inquires in
the most approved style:

"What name shall I say?" though, as I have seen
her scores of times when she was attending school, I
fancy my face must be as familiar to those round eyes
of hers as the steeple of Thornleigh Church.

But she has been carefully drilled, and must do
credit to her instructress.

After a quarter of an hour's conversation with the
latter, I take my leave: it has been rather fatiguing
work, as I have had to originate all the remarks,
receiving merely monosyllabic replies. We are most
genteel, both of us, but on the whole I prefer the
ordinary style of conversation at Thornleigh—about
ailments, and babies, and pigs, and how I myself am
not as young as I used to be, and how they hope I'll
not take it amiss, but raly I am sadly warsening. A
body couldn't but notice it—that kind o' stoop now
that I seem to be gettin'. But, eh well! we're all
gettin' on, aren't we?

"OUR JOE"

As old Harry Lupton wended his way homewards on Christmas Eve he began to think seriously of writing to his son in America, and desiring him to come back to

England forthwith. Every house in the village was astir with preparations for family gatherings; here and there, indeed, were travellers already arriving—sons and daughters home from service, or snatching a holiday

from "business" in the neighbouring market town. Some—and these were not the least welcome—brought only little bundles in their hands; but others carried hampers filled with good things (at sight of which there was a fine outcry among the small fry in the household); and others, again, dragged little tired children slowly along, or bore them in their arms. Then, when the door was opened, and "grandma's" cheery wrinkled face peered out into the night, what jubilee there was! How Billy was promised a treacle-butty immediately if he would "give over" his fretful wail; how much Nelly (bless her heart!) was declared to have "come on;" and what a marvellous likeness was discovered between the new baby and its father. Harry Lupton, picking his way over the cobble-stones slowly enough—for his lumbaguey catched him awful, and his legs was none so strong as they were—noted all this bustle, and there came a mist before his eyes other than that of the gathering dusk, and a chill about his heart which was not caused by the fast-falling flakes of snow, or the cutting evening wind. When he turned up the little dark lane which led to his cottage—the last in the village, and a couple of hundred yards away from any of the neighbouring homesteads—he was obliged to stand still for a moment and cough—there was such a disagreeable sensation in his throat—and pass his hand across his eyes.

" It's gettin' time for our Joe to be thinkin' o' comin' home. Our Alice must write an' tell him. Her an' me's gettin' on—we might be in we're graves next Christmas, an' then theer'd be no use in him comin' at all. I'll bid her write—I will."

He nodded confidentially to the hedges, and toddled on again, his tall bent figure and feeble gait pathetically endorsing his words.

In a few minutes he had reached his abode, a queer little two-storeyed cottage built of yellowish stone. Light shone through the small-paned windows and a cheerful glow irradiated the figure of the old woman who stood on the threshold.

"Eh, ye're awful late, 'Arry! I couldn't think whatever'd come to ye. Your back that bad, an' all."

"Come in, missis, come in, an' shut yon door; theer's wind enough to blow th' teeth out o' yer 'ead— if ye had any, that's to say. Come, that's better! Coffee smells first-rate. Off wi' th' clogs! Help us into the cheer, missus; e-e-ch, it do come same as a knife in a body's back, that plaguey sciatic' when one goes for to sit down. Theer! all's well as ends well. Now th' bacon, an' th' toast. Theer! I'm feelin' a bit better now."

He drew his elbow-chair nearer to the fire, and fell to at his supper, a brighter expression coming over his face, and his melancholy thoughts banished for the time. Indeed it would have been hard to feel melancholy in that cosy little kitchen while the firelight danced so cheerily over the creamy walls and well-rubbed furniture, and brought to view such a wealth of brilliantly coloured crockery, and so many glittering pots and pans. Mrs. Alice Lupton had nothing to do but "keep the place clean," and was scrubbing, and rubbing, and polishing from morning till night. Her own figure was very pleasant to look at, in its tidy north-country dress. She was a pretty old woman, good-tempered and thrifty; and any one, seeing her as she sat smiling at her good man from the opposite side of the fireplace, would have felt that he was rather to be envied than pitied. After a few minutes, however, he heaved a deep sigh, and laid down his knife.

"What's to do wi' ye?" asked Alice anxiously.

"I've been thinkin' a dale of our Joe to-neet, missus, an' I was sayin' to mysel' as it were gettin' time for him to be comin' home. Ye might write him a line an' tell him as his feyther says so."

"Well, master," returned Mrs. Lupton, rubbing her nose reflectively, "I don't altogether know if we didn't ought to let th' lad bide till he comes of hissel'. Ye see, every letter tells us as he's doin' pretty fair, an' that; an' happen it 'ud be a pity to take him off's work just because we want to look at him."

"Let's see, he's been a matter o' sixteen year out yonder, han't he? He's a man now; aye, goin' on thirty-four he is, an' ought to ha' laid by summat—a steady hard-working lad same as he's been. He ought to ha' saved a tidy bit, enough to keep's feyther an' mother i' their owd age. We're gettin' on, missus: ye're that 'earty still ye make no count o' the time; but I'm gettin' past work, an' I say as it's time our Joe come an' worked *for* us. Theer!"

He hammered on the table with his fist, and nodded at his wife in a way which betokened that he had said the last word on the subject.

She was pondering a little anxiously as to the advisability of carrying out his wish, when there came a knock, or rather a series of knocks, at the door.

"Whoever can it be at this time o' th' neet?" growled Harry. "Go an' see, missus; I'm too crippled to stir."

Mrs. Lupton left the kitchen and opened the house-door, starting a little at the sight of the man's figure which confronted her.

"Can I—will you kindly let me come in and warm myself for a few minutes? I am drenched through, and so cold and numb."

"It's a tramping chap, I doubt," said Alice in a

whisper, as she returned to her husband, " but it 'ud be a charity to let him come in for a bit. He looks for all the world like a ghost."

" Let him in then—though I'm none so fond o' tramps. But Christmas Eve a body mustn't be too 'ard. Come in, mister, an' sit ye down. It's an awful neet."

The stranger entered—a tall man who might have been good-looking but for the unhealthy pallor of his face, the sharpened outlines of his features, the stoop in his broad shoulders, and the stubbly beard on his chin. His clothes, besides being ragged, were soaked with melted snow and smeared with mud. Harry glanced at him with much disfavour, and edged away his chair a little; but Alice fetched him a plate, and presently desired him to comfort his inner man with bacon and buttered toast, while she warmed up a cup of coffee.

" Ye'll have come a long way, I reckon?" observed Harry after a pause.

" Aye, I've walked from Liverpool."

" An' afore that?"

" I sailed from New York."

" New York, eh dear! that's wheer our Joe lives," cried Alice eagerly. " I do wonder if ye ever come across our Joe—our son that is, as has been there these sixteen year. Joe Lupton from Thornleigh. Did ye know him?"

The stranger was silent for a moment, stirring vigorously at his coffee, and seeming to reflect.

"Joe Lupton," he said slowly, at last. "New York's such a big place—I know a lot of English fellows. Let's see, what was he like?"

"Eh, a tall slip of a lad wi' rosy cheeks, same as two ripe apples, and hair that curly! D'ye mind, master, how 't 'ud twine round th' comb of a Saturday, when our Joe was a little 'un, an' I'd washed him i' th' dolly-tub? Eh, dear 'eart, he was a bonny child!"

"Why, missus, a tall lad wi' rosy cheeks! What sort of a description's that?" chuckled Harry. "They women, they all'ays thinks as time stands still. Our Joe'll be a man now, wi' a fine pair of shoulders I reckon, an' a gradely beard to's face. But I'll tell'ee, mister. He had a pair o' blue eyes, bright an' clear, as could look a man straight i' th' face, he had; and an honest kind of a way wi' him as made ye feel he was a lad ye could trust. Did ye know any one o' that make yonder, o' th' name o' Joe, from Thornleigh?"

There was a silence for a little time again, and then the man shook his head.

"No," he said. "I don't know anybody o' th' kind. But you see he might be there an' yet I mightn't come across him."

"Ah," sighed Alice, deeply disappointed. "New

York's a big place, as ye say. Is't a place, d'ye think, wheer folks get's on?"

"Ah, that's it," put in Harry; "is it a place wheer folks makes much money?"

The stranger broke into a short laugh. "Oh, aye! money enough!" he said, and buried his face in his cup.

"Didn't I tell'ee?" cried old Lupton, nodding triumphantly at Alice. "Our Joe'll have saved a tidy bit. Eh, happen ye'll be ridin' to church i' yer own trap afore ye dee, owd wench!"

There was a sound as of a sudden explosion in the stranger's coffee-cup, at which lack of politeness his host was mightily indignant.

"It's very fine for ye to laugh," he remarked, "an' yet theer's nought to laugh at as I can see. Our Joe's been workin' 'ard for sixteen year, an' I say he ought to ha' saved enough to keep us i' comfort—his mother an' me. He should come back, he should. Missus, ye mun write and tell him that to-morrow."

"Ah!" sighed the traveller, "I'm longin' sorely to see *my* old father an' mother. I'm homesick, an' yet I dursen't go home."

"Why?" cried Alice in surprise, while Harry paused, pipe in hand, to look up inquiringly.

"Ye see I've been in a bit of a mess," answered the man hesitatingly. "In fact, I've seen a sight o' trouble since first I went out yonder, as a young chap. I got into bad ways, an' fell in with a bad lot, and—the long and the short of it is, I've just put in five years for burglary."

"Eh, dear heart!" ejaculated Alice, much startled. Harry half rose from his chair, and stretched out his hand towards his big stick.

"Nay, missus, don't be frightened o' me," cried the stranger eagerly. "I swear I'd rather die than touch a hair o' your head. You've no need.to reach for your stick, sir," he added, turning to his host. "Is it likely I'd tell you my misfortunes if I wanted to harm you? I'm thinkin' of my own parents this blessed night, an' wonderin' if I'll ever have the courage to own what I've done, and to ax their forgiveness."

His voice shook, and he shaded his eyes with his hand.

"Eh, dear heart!" said Mrs. Lupton again. "Don't they know, then? Poor souls! it'll go 'ard wi' 'em, I doubt."

"It will," said the man with something like a sob. "No, they know nothing; I kep' it from them, for I knew it 'ud go nigh to kill them. You see they come of honest stock, an' have always held up their heads pretty high. All the neighbours think well o' them, an' respect them. So I've always wrote as I was doin' well, an' the chaplain yonder was very good to me, an' used to post my letters an' bring me the replies.

They're but simple folk; an' never guessed as there were anything wrong. God knows I'm loth to be the means o' bringin' shame to them now. An' yet I'm the only son they have!"

Alice clapped her withered hands together, and rocked herself to and fro in her chair.

"God preserve us! what trouble some folks has!— Eh, what awful trouble! I doubt they'll break their 'earts, when they come to 'ear."

The stranger held his peace for a moment. Old Harry removed his pipe, and stared at him with increasing dislike and disapproval.

"I'm loth to bring shame to 'em," repeated the man at last from behind his sheltering hand. "Maybe, after all, it 'ud be best for me not to go near 'em.

Maybe I'd better go back where I came from an' tell 'em nothing."

"Ye're reet theer," said Harry, sternly. "To my thinkin' ye'd best go away an' keep away, lad. What for should ye go home to disgrace yer feyther an' mother i' their owd age—them as is decent folks, ye say? T'ave th' neighbours castin' up at 'em, as their son was a thief, an' was i' jail five year? Why t'ud kill 'em straight off, I shouldn't wonder. Nay, nay, go back wheer ye've comed from, an' try to lead an honest life—that's my advice."

"Aye," returned the other, almost in a whisper, "I'll go back an' try to lead an honest life."

"Ah, but I reckon your mother 'ud like to see ye," cried Alice; "I reckon she would if it was ever so. But men folks is different. They're a deal harder, an' yet they can't bear trouble same as us. 'Twould go nigh to kill yer feyther, th' shame an' the sorrow would. Happen, ye'd best do as my master advises, arter all."

The man's other hand went up to his face now, and his voice sounded husky and unsteady as he said: "Thank ye, I will—I'll go." Then dropping his hands, he rose.

Alice's eyes filled with tears.

"Nay, but theer's no such hurry," she said, "an' th' neet's bad for travellin'. Ye'd best stop here, an' go on i' th' mornin'."

" Ah, theer's th' shippon," added her husband, rather unwilling; "an' a good bit o' straw. Ye might make shift on't for bed. It's better nor th' snow anyways."

"'Thank ye kindly," said the stranger. "It is so; I'm pleased to have the chance."

His eyes, which had hitherto shifted uneasily from one object to another when they were not bent on the ground, now swept round the room with a long steady glance, resting for a moment or two on the stooping figure of the old man in the corner. He made a step towards him with hand half extended, but meeting Harry's severe gaze, drew back, and nodded instead.

Alice lit a candle and preceded him out of the room, carefully closing the door after her.

" Hark," she whispered when they stood without. " Ye needn't sleep i' th' shippon when all's said an' done. Theer's a bit of a room here near th' stairs wheer our Joe used to sleep. I've all'ays kep' it tidy, an' bed ready aired; it seems to comfort me, you know, an' I think to mysel' sometimes, happen he'll come an' surprise us some day, an' he must find all ready. Ye can sleep theer—the master needn't know."

It was a queer little cupboard of a room into which Mrs. Lupton ushered him, containing just a truckle-bed, a chair beside it, and a chest of drawers with a jug and basin on the top. The man sat down on the chair, as though seized with sudden faintness, but his hostess was too busy with her preparations for his comfort to notice him.

"Little did I think as I'd ever let a trampin' chap same as you sleep in our Joe's bed. But I'm sorry for ye, an' that's the truth. I doubt ye took it 'ard o' my master to speak like he did. But theer! men's ways *are* 'ard, an' my master is all'ays so set on honesty."

She had put on sheets and blankets, smoothed and patted them, and was now shaking a pillow into its coarse clean cover. When she had finished and laid it in its place she suddenly stooped and kissed it.

Turning and catching her guest's eyes, and observing the strange expression of his face, she blushed to her very cap borders.

"I doubt ye'll think me a queer sort of body," she said. "But it's a way I've got whenever I come next or nigh this bed. Ye see I all'ays think o' our Joe's bonny face as I used to see it, mornin' an' evenin', laying on this here pillow, an' as I can't kiss that, I kiss th' pillow i'stead."

The man uttered a sort of groan and flung himself forward on the bed, clutching the pillow with both hands, and burying his face in it.

"Poor fellow!" murmured Alice, "Ye're thinkin' o' yer own mother I reckon."

At this juncture Harry's voice was heard angrily

calling, and the tap of his stick came across the floor of the adjoining room.

Alice hastily extinguished the candle, and crept into the passage, artfully banging the house door as though she had just come in.

" Whatever ha' ye been doin' out i' th' cold so long ? " cried her lord, emerging from the kitchen in much displeasure.

" I were but makin' yon poor chap a bit comfortable," returned Alice.

" I'm none too sure as ye did reet to let 'im bide here at all," said Harry. " I don't so much care for folks o' that mak' about th' place. Whish ! seems as if I could smell th' prison off him ! "

Slowly the heavy feet and the tapping stick passed the stranger's door; he had heard every word the old man said, and now burrowed his head yet more deeply into the pillow, and groaned afresh.

Mrs. Lupton, excited and compassionate, lay awake long after her master's snores made the very rafters ring, and at last, dropping to sleep towards morning, was troubled by a strange and painful dream.

She thought she saw their Joe, a child again with rosy face and curly head; and he stood without in the snow and wept, and his father drove him from the door. The vision was so vivid, she saw the little lad so plainly, with the tears on his chubby cheeks and his mouth drawn downwards in the pitiful droop against which so few mothers can steel their hearts, that when she woke she could hardly believe it was not real.

" 'Twas wi' moiderin' about yon poor fellow, I doubt," she said to herself, and lay still, the memory of her dream mingling with the thought of the tramp, until she fell into a sort of waking nightmare, in which it seemed to her that her son and the tramp were one. Presently she started up, fully conscious and struck with a sudden fear—a fear more terrible than that evoked by any nightmare—which made her heart stand still and her hands turn cold. What if they *were* one? What if this "tramping chap," this jail-bird, were really their Joe?

With awful clearness the stranger's story returned to her mind: she went over it phrase by phrase, word by word. There was nothing, nothing in his history which might not—admitting the fact that it were possible for Joe to have gone astray—have also befallen him. She remembered the tremulous speech, the downcast looks, the emotion of their visitor; and the fear grew upon her, and shook her very soul. She sprang out of bed, while Harry snored on peacefully; the dawn showed grey through the uncurtained windows, and the wind whistled without. She flung a shawl over her shoulders and pattered downstairs, the boards icy-cold to her bare feet, the chill air that circled through the house, seeming to penetrate even to her bones.

The door was ajar, and through it was to be seen a vision of a desolate white world, with never a living  creature stirring; only a long irregular line of hedge, and trees standing out, gaunt and black, against a lowering sky.

Alice caught her breath, and leaned against the door-post for a moment. Then supporting herself against the wall, and breaking into a stifled, piteous whimpering, she crept into Joe's little room. Lo! it was empty. The bed had not been slept in, but the pillow was crushed and soiled, and there, in the middle, where the mother's lips had touched it, it was wet, as though with tears.

MATES

THE Squire of Thornleigh, though willing enough to conform to modern ideas on certain subjects, retains to this day many old-fashioned notions with regard to sport. He will persist in looking at it as a matter of pleasure, not profit; therefore he never endeavours to make Thornleigh shooting " pay."

He employs a certain number of keepers, and rears a certain number of pheasants, and he and his friends shoot them at their leisure, and as many as are wanted for " the house " are kept and the rest given away. It never occurs to him to sell so much as a feather of them.

" A shoot " at Thornleigh is a pleasant business even for the non-sporting members of the community. The bustle and stir, the tramping of heavy boots, the ecstatic barking of dogs, the hunting for somebody's flask, and the filling of some one else's tobacco-pouch ; the animated discussion as to *where* lunch is to be ; the procession across the stable-yard to the gun-room,

251

where the two chief keepers wait solemn and expectant; the gathering together of a little army of beaters; there is a certain excitement about it all which infects even the most tender-hearted of the ladies.

Now for the guns!

"Billy, you old villain, you haven't touched mine since I used it on Friday! The barrels are like factory chimneys."

"I beg your pardon, Mester Edward. I cleaned it o' Saturday. Ye must ha' taken it out wi'out tellin' me since."

"So I did— when I went after those ducks at the Mosses. It's all right, old chap."

"Now, is everybody ready? We ought to have started ages ago. It will be dark before we know where we are. *Is* every one here?"

"Squire's not comed yet."

"Not here? No, he isn't. What *is* he doing? Do go and see what he's about, somebody."

Somebody goes, and presently returns with the announcement that the Squire has not begun to put on his boots yet. There is a general groan.

" Then we sha'n't get off for *hours*," said one resigned voice, and the butt-end of a gun rings on the pavement: consternation is painted on every face — everybody knows what the Squire's boots are.

Presently a breathless messenger arrives from the house—" He's getting them on !" and then comes a

girl, jubilant—" Papa's nearly ready !" And finally
the Squire himself appears, sauntering leisurely along,
placidly asserting that there's " lots of time," and
pausing as he passes the stables to strike a match on
the wall, and to light his pipe in the most imperturbable
manner possible.

It is not that he is less keen a sportsman than the
very youngest of the party, but he is accustomed to
look on time as an elastic commodity, and sees no
reason why he should take the edge off his enjoyment
by hurrying. At last he is under weigh; he has got
his gun and his cartridge-bag and his game-bag; he
has searched all his pockets to make sure that his
match-box and tobacco-pouch are safe; he has sent one
of his daughters to the house for his pocket-handkerchief;
he has discussed the prospects of sport with the head-
keeper, and patted the dogs and secured his own special
favourite—a young black retriever—by a stout thong
to the belt round his waist. Finally, just as the
general impatience has reached fever-height, he remarks
that he thinks it is about time to be moving, and off
they go; the retriever straining at his collar, and
ready, at the first rabbit which crosses his path, to tow
his master half across a field. The Squire says this dog
is " half-broken "—he has one or two little pet theories
of the kind, such as that the most infantine of the
rabbits against which he wages unrelenting war on

account of the damage they do to his holly-trees, is "three-parts grown," and that any animal in the stables, from the old hack on which all his girls have learnt to ride, to a three-year-old colt, is "well up to" his weight.

The womankind return to the house. If the home coverts are to be gone through, one or two of the younger ones may presently follow the sportsmen (I must own that my own enthusiasm never stood this test); or if the party is going further afield, we shall probably meet them at some farmhouse or keeper's hut with luncheon; "hot-pot" being one of the standing dishes on these occasions. It is amusing, if one arrives first at the rendezvous, to watch the faces of the sportsmen as they come straggling in; one can tell by the first glance how the day has gone with them. The complacency of some, the depression of others—neophytes these; easy unconcern marks the practised hand who "couldn't miss if he tried;" while the gloom of "the fellow who let slip the only woodcock we saw," would be noticeable even if the Squire did not announce in a stage whisper that one might as well take him out with a walking-stick. Luncheon, however, revives drooping spirits, and further invigorates hopeful ones; anecdotes are told amid much laughter, and there is some good-humoured chaffing, good-humouredly taken.

Without, the keepers and beaters discuss various matters over their solid viands. Strong ale warms old Billy's heart and loosens his tongue. He relates certain reminiscences; recalling bygone encounters with poachers, with half-contemptuous comments on the "softness" of lads of the present day, which make one or two of the underlings hang their heads; and winds up with his favourite story of the last time the Squire of Upton came to shoot at Thornleigh.

"He were a queer 'un," says Billy, "t'owd Squire of Upton. I niver see such a one. He wouldn't never have no big shoots at Upton yonder, same as we've allus had here. He didn't seem to care to 'ave parties o' gentry stoppin' i' th' house. 'Nay, nay,' says th' owd Squire, 'fish an' strangers stink arter three days.' Eh, he was a queer 'un! Well, one day we was patrick-shootin' 'ere, an' he coom out wi' us: he'd do that sometimes when he'd a mind, though he didn't care for other folks going ower yonder. It were mortal hot, an' i' th' arternoon a storm coom, wi' thunder an' leetnin' an' a downpour o' rain as drenched us afore we could get shelter. We was all makin' here an' there, an' nobody noticed wheer Squire of Upton had getten to; but arter a bit, when storm was ower an' we was all makin' whoam as wet as water-dogs, he nips out on us from a field o' turmits t'other side o' th' hedge.

"'Hallo!' says the Squire, stoppin' an' givin' hiinsel' a bit of a shake, for the water was runnin' off him.

"'Hallo agen,' says Squire of Upton. 'Ye seem a bit wet,' says he.

"'I should think I *was* wet,' says Squire. 'Aren't you?'

"'Nay, nought to speak on,' says t'owd gentleman laughin' to himsel'. 'Ye should ha' done same as me,' says he.

"'What's that?' says the Squire.

"'Why,' says Squire of Upton. 'I took off my clothes an' sat on 'em.'"

This story is received with applause and laughter, and then Billy, the other old keeper, relates how he caught that famous "snig" in one of the dykes yonder, when he was a young 'un.

Never was such an eel as that; it was caught about fifty years ago, but has been growing ever since. Each time Billy "unbethinks himsel'" about it, its length increases, and there is every reason to believe it will rival the sea-serpent before he has done with it.

Presently another voice strikes in: "Ye'll have heerd owd Betty yonder at the lone-end is gone?"

"Eh, is she?" respond the hearers in different tones of regret.

"She were a kind o' cousin o' my own," adds Billy, "an' a decent 'ard-workin' owd body. Ye'll miss her goin' your round, Bob. Ye mind how she was allus sat aside o' th' road watchin' her cow, an' knittin'.'"

"Ah, I do," replies old Bob, whose beat takes him past the "lone-end" every day of his life. "Poor owd Betty! Jim'll be in a terrible way. She was near th' end when I looked in yesterday, an' poor owd Jim was pattin' her o' th' hand an' tellin' her to keep her 'eart up. Theer was th' two o' them lyin' one aside o' t'other, an' th' owd woman deein' fast, an' Jim reachin' ower to her an' pattin' her, an' axin' 'How are ye now, owd lady? D'ye find yoursel' any more comfortable?' An' she deein'!"

"Eh, th' poor owd chap's gettin' a bit silly," says some one, presumably the small farmer in whose house the party is assembled. "He's old, ye know, an's been bedridden this many year. Eh, 'twas the wonderfullest thing to 'ear him this mornin' arter the owd woman was gone, an' they were talkin' o' shiftin' her—for 'twas a strange thing to 'ave her theer lyin' aside o' Jim an' she dead. An' wheer should they lay her out? they was sayin'—there is but two rooms in yon little house, ye know, an' Alice the daughter sleeps in th' only bed they have besides th' owd folks'. 'Ye've no need to shift her at all,' says Jim. 'I can do wi' her here,' he says. 'I wunnot have her taken away,' says he; an' then he

reaches out his hand an' strokes her. 'Eh, missus,' he
says, 'I'm fain to keep ye as long as I can. They mun
let ye bide to th' last,' he says. Eh, I thought it was
the wonderfullest thing!"

"Ah, poor Jim!" says Bob, "I'm sorry for th' owd
chap. He'll be lost without his missus. But I reckon
he'll not be so longer arter her."

"Aye, he'll soon be aside of her again," responds
Billy, and then there is a scraping of feet and a general
move—the mid-day meal is over.

In the evening the result of the day's sport is laid out
for general inspection, pheasants, hares, wild duck, a few
rabbits, perhaps a water-hen or two, and—with good
luck, for they are scarce in these parts—a couple of
woodcocks.

Well, the day is done, and on the whole every one
is well satisfied; "the gentry" come in, pleasantly
tired, to refresh themselves with tea, or whatever
their "particular vanity" may be; the beaters and
underlings melt away; and last of all Billy and
Bob turn their steps homewards, one walking a little
in front of the other, according to time-honoured
custom.

Never was there a pair more truly attached to one
another than this brace of "mates," though Billy is
tenacious of his prerogative as chief, and Bob takes his
orders with becoming humility.

Bob would as soon think of arguing with the head-keeper as of walking alongside of him. Argument indeed or conversation of any kind does not seem to occur to either of them, though they spend hours in each other's company: except on the occasion of a big "do," when for the honour of the thing they are bound to exert themselves, they are a taciturn couple—Billy is taciturn, even in his cups, as a rule, though once he aroused the Squire at dawn of day by throwing pebbles against his window and requesting him to come down forthwith and help him to rout a very army of poachers which he declared were overrunning the park. Billy had a great deal to say about these poachers. "Town poachers, they were," he assured the Squire, and of the most malignant order: even when the depredators turned out to be sheep, Billy's angry loquaciousness could not be checked. But as a rule there never were such silent and cheerless "sprees" as those in which he periodically indulges. He sits sighing and shaking his head at the fire, and remorsefully "fuddling himself" day after day, a most melancholy spectacle.

The objurgations of his wife are of no avail; the remonstrances and persuasions of the Canon fall alike unheeded. Squire is the only one who "can get any good o' Billy" under these circumstances, and even he has to wait till Billy is "ripe for it."

I was much astonished once, being still new to
Thornleigh and Thornleigh ways, when a stalwart
youth in corduroys flew past me, hastily observing to
the Canon, with whom I was chatting outside the church
porch, that he was "goin for Squire for feyther." A
short time after, the Squire appeared, pipe in mouth,
stick in hand, retriever at heel, and escorted by the
anxious messenger, on his way to lecture Billy. And in
a few days Billy resumed work, very solemn and severe
in manner, if a little shaky about the legs. I soon
became used to this course of events.

During the periodical "bouts" of his chief, Bob takes
refuge in a stolid affectation of innocence.

"Billy's not so well," he remarks, if questioned,
though every child in the place knows the reason of
Billy's indisposition, and though Bob makes a point of
sitting with him in the evenings, watching his potations
with gloomy dissatisfaction, but never "offering to say
a word."

Once Billy got "the titus," or "brown-titus"—as
bronchitis is indifferently called in Thornleigh—while
he was still weak after an outbreak, and for a time was
very seriously ill. Bob's distress was touching to
witness. He "moidered" Billy's wife, and occasionally
irritated the invalid himself by his repeated inquiries;
and once when offered a glass of ale by way of consolation he heaved a deep sigh, and observed that if his

mate went, he didn't care if he never got "a wet" again. Spoken thus with tears in his blue eyes, and his weather-beaten old face all puckered with grief and anxiety, this remark of Bob's was genuinely pathetic. However, he has luckily not yet been called upon to become a teetotaller: Billy "mended" in course of time, and Bob follows his lead as of yore. The old white heads are both getting rather bent and the broad velveteen-clad shoulders stoop a little; Billy is "going" at the knees, and Bob drags one foot slightly as he walks. One feels a little pang as one watches them. Joseph, too, told me the other day that he was "wearin' away;" and Robert, whose "winter cough" has been very bad of late made some jocular remark on the subject of his coffin, which betrayed the bent of his thoughts.

The curtain has risen on the last act of this bucolic play, and the chorus of old men's voices grows fainter as they make their exit one by one. Soon the drop scene will fall, and the stage will be cleared for younger, more energetic actors.

There is a certain likeness to their fathers in the new generation: certain tricks of manner, certain tones of voice: but there is much that is strange. Yet a few years, and it may be that Thornleigh itself will be altered and modernised beyond recognition, its old-fashioned customs forgotten, its traditions stamped out. The old order changeth, and the fashion of this world passeth away; but when the time comes for Thornleigh to be "improved" and civilised, may I not be there to see!

Printed by BALLANTYNE, HANSON & Co.
London & Edinburgh